PENGUIN BOOK
ARJUN

Sunil Gangopadhyay was born in Faridpur, Bangladesh, in 1934 and educated at Calcutta University. While still a student he founded a poetry magazine and has devoted himself to writing prose and poetry ever since. In 1963 he participated in the International Writers Workshop Program at Iowa State University.

His first novel *Atmaprakash* was published in 1966. Two of his novels *The Adversary* and *Days and Nights in the Forest* have been filmed by Satyajit Ray and his most recent novel *Those Times* was awarded the Sahitya Akademi Award. Sunil Gangopadhyay lives in Calcutta where he edits the poetry section of *Desh* magazine. He is married and has one son.

*

Chitrita Banerji-Abdullah was born in 1947 and was educated at Presidency College, Calcutta, and Harvard University. She has worked for various development agencies as well as for a publishing firm in America. She has translated Bengali short stories into English for literary magazines and the BBC.

She lives at present in Calcutta.

ARJUN

Sunil Gangopadhyay

Translated from the Bengali
by Chitrita Banerji-Abdullah

PENGUIN BOOKS

Penguin Books (India) Private Ltd., 72-B Himalaya House, 23 Kasturba Gandhi
Marg, New Delhi-110 001, India.
Penguin Books Ltd, Harmondsworth, Middlesex, England
Viking Penguin Inc., 40 West 23rd Street, New York, New York 10010, U.S.A.
Penguin Books Australia Ltd, Ringwood, Victoria, Australia
Penguin Books Canada Ltd, 2801 John Street, Markham, Ontario, Canada L3R 1B4
Penguin Books (N.Z.) Ltd, 182-190 Wairau Road, Auckland 10, New Zealand

First Published in Bengali by Ananda Publishers Private Limited 1971
Published in Penguin Books 1987
Copyright © Penguin Books (India) Private Limited 1987
All Rights Reserved

Made and Printed in India by
Ananda Offset Private Limited, Calcutta.
Typeset in Olympian

ARJUN

ARJUN

Translator's Preface

It is always difficult to convey the nuances and flavour of an original work in a translation. This becomes doubly difficult when there is a transition between two such widely disparate languages as Bengali and English. Added to this, there is the difficulty of depicting a South Asian culture in a western language without an imbalance, either in accuracy or in immediacy. *Arjun*, however, has an additional dimension which is obvious to the average Bengali reader (or for that matter, the average Indian reader), but which needs to be explained briefly to the western reader.

In its basic outline, this book is based on the main story of the Indian epic, the *Mahabharata*. In fact, the name of the protagonist in the novel, Arjun, is the same as that of one character—perhaps the most heroic one—in the epic. The *Mahabharata* follows the fortunes of the five Pandava brothers who, being fatherless, are cheated of their rightful inheritance by their wicked and powerful cousins, the Kauravas. After many years of hardship, many escapes from death and several abortive attempts at peaceful negotiations for their share of the kingdom the Pandavas, with their followers and allies, finally meet the mighty Kauravas in war, on the battlefield of Kurukshetra. Their one great asset, apart from their heroism, fortitude and virtue, is the friendship between Arjun and Krishna, one of the incarnations of Vishnu, the second of the Hindu Trinity. It is because of this friendship that Krishna decides to drive Arjun's chariot in battle for him.

However, when Arjun does come on to the field and sees his own cousins· as well as many former friends and relatives arrayed in battle against him, he is totally unmanned—not out of fear, for Arjun has proved himself to be fearless; but because of infinite sadness and revulsion at the thought of slaughtering all these people. How can a kingdom be worth it? He is so overcome, that he drops all his weapons and sits down in the chariot, refusing to fight.

That is when Krishna speaks to him about his duty as a warrior in a magnificent combination of exhortation, entreaty and command as well as a profound analysis of religion and ethics (which has become known as the *Bhagavad Gita*). Finally Arjun realizes that he must sacrifice personal feelings of attachment and compunction, take hold of himself and fight to the best of his ability as a warrior—because this is a just cause. And so, after great acts of individual heroism on both sides, the battle of Kurukshetra does end in victory for Arjun and his brothers, a victory for right and justice.

But in a novel about the struggle for survival in the twentieth century, no god can be invoked to come down and lead the hero to a glorious victory. Nor are the issues of conflict of epic proportions. Nevertheless, the latter-day Arjun does find his destiny in a way similar to that of his namesake. After vain attempts at settlement through rational discussion, though without giving up one's basic rights, this Arjun also leads his followers into battle. The sight of familiar faces among the enemy debilitates and emasculates him too for a time. But the wanton killing of a pet dog brings home the futility of expecting fair play or kindness from people whose greed for possession is overwhelming. So Arjun, the man of intellect and of peace, is roused to become the fearless, rage-filled, larger-than-life hero who will fight, and fight to win.

I would like to thank Abu Abdullah, F.K. Ghuznavi, and Lawrence Lifschultz for their encouragement and moral support during the period when *Arjun* was being translated.

Chitrita Banerji-Abdullah
Cambridge, Massachusetts, 1986

I

Take a good look at that girl. You cannot see her very clearly, of course, since it is much too dark. The electricity has just gone off in their house, in the whole neighbourhood. But she just keeps on sitting with her books in the faint hope that the lights will come back on. She is about twenty-one, her long hair hanging down in a braid. Look, it is becoming easier to see things in the dark now. The pale glow of a growing moon filters through the open window.

There are no chairs or tables in the room. She has been working on her bed with books and papers scattered all around her. She occasionally bites her pen, an old habit with her. Irritated by the continuing darkness, she steps down from the bed and goes over to the window. She does not have much beauty, but of health she has a fair share. A light brown complexion. Not having had to go out all day, her sari is draped casually around her. Her name...

From the next room, her mother calls, 'Labi, where is the candle?'

You don't like this name, Labi, do you? Her parents, her grandfather, even her neighbours, call her Labi. In college, however, she is known as Labonya.* Her BA finals are only seventeen days away; discontent mars the symmetry of her eyebrows at the defection of the power supply. It is about eight-thirty in the evening. In the Dum Dum area where Labonya lives, such power cuts are quite frequent, their duration completely uncertain. Yet

---

* Labonya: an approximate English equivalent of the word is 'grace'.

11

how unjust. There has been no storm today to fell a tree and pull out the electric wires. Of course, it is also a fact that even a year ago, Labonya's house did not have a power connection. But within that time, the lanterns and oil lamps all seem to have disappeared.

A general hullabaloo was heard as soon as the power went off—everybody starting to speak at the same time. But now it is deathly quiet. In the weak, pallid moonlight, a poor adversary to the darkness, the whole neighbourhood seems colourless, lifeless. As if it is waiting to come back to life at the touch of a magic wand.

*

In her cramped little room, Labonya continued to fret with unease and irritation. A mynah thrashing about in its cage was what she reminded one of. One could not call Labonya beautiful, but she had a fine pair of eyes. When she was unhappy, or when she concentrated on some thought, her eyes acquired a darkness and a depth, and her face was illuminated with a touch of grace. Most people could never see this. But her father had been able to perceive it, which was why he had called her Labonya. But the girl was too headstrong. Anger, rather than sorrow, was her dominant passion. Her conduct at most times did not fit in with the softness of her formal name. Then she was no longer Labonya, just plain Labi.

Her mother enquired a couple more times about the candle. But Labonya did not answer. She brought her braided hair over in front and started to twine it round and round her finger. Her mother, not hearing her daughter answer, stopped asking. Labonya only responded when she felt like it. To ask too often would only make her lash out in a temper. Even though there was no fan in the room, sudden darkness always made you feel the heat more. Labonya sensed beads of sweat appearing on her forehead.

Shortly after her mother's voice stopped Labonya herself started looking for the candle. There was no particular likelihood of the candle being in the room, and that too under the bed; but Labonya crawled under, just the same. She was alone in the room, it would not matter much if her clothes got into immodest disarray. It was even darker under the bed. She had failed in her finals last year. At this moment all she was thinking of was that she had to pass this year, just had to. And yet, the lights kept going off, time and again.

She let out an exclamation of disgust at not being able to find the candle after all. In this room now, there was this girl all by herself, a girl who had health rather than beauty, who badly wanted to pass her exams—throbbing with irritation. She simply could not bear the darkness.

Labonya walked over and stood by the window again. Her braid was pulled forward, her fingers habitually twining in it. Naturally enough, the darkness was lighter outside. There was electricity in all the houses on the other side of the street. The two neighbourhoods faced each other, one dark, the other illuminated.

There was a frame for the climbing gourd plant, and a grapefruit tree in front of the house. Labonya saw her grandfather, Nishinath, going out towards the road, leaning on her eleven-year-old brother Naru's shoulder. Did the old man have to go out now, just when there was a power cut? He stumbled once, on a brick lying on the ground.

Labonya's eyes moved in another direction. Two shadowy figures had appeared. She made them out soon enough. At first, they seemed like two flying sparks of fire, for both of them lighted cigarettes. Then she saw the hands, the face, the rest of the body. Sukhen and Dibya. The two stopped suddenly. Usually, a natural instinct would make them both look at Labonya's window at least once. She moved aside a little, so as to avoid meeting their eyes, and drew her sari more carefully over herself. Let us leave her standing there for the present and look at these two young men. Sukhen was about thirty-two, but did not look more than twenty-two or twenty-three, with his thin, wiry body. He did not have much of a beard either. A few more years of youthfulness were left to him. He sang well, but he also worked in a bakery—a point he made quite often to his other unemployed friends.

13

Dibya had once been runner-up in the junior group of the All Bengal Wrestling Competition. He had not won the title because he hadn't learnt all the tricks of his art properly. But, in a contest of sheer physical strength, all the other competitors would have been as mere children to him. He was not built like the usual wrestler, either. There was not an ounce of superfluous fat on his body. His complexion was fair, his height a respectable five-foot-eleven inches. Had there not been a hardness to his features, he could well have been considered handsome. In childhood and in boyhood, when the softness had still lingered in his face, that beautifully fashioned body of his had made him look like a cherub.

The two of them, Sukhen and Dibya, flung their cigarette butts away at the same time.

'Three times a week', said Sukhen, 'the power has to go off. How long does one put up with this?'

'Yes,' said Dibya, 'they are all out to get us these days.'

This piece of land, where the colony had grown, was elevated quite a bit from the level of the main road. At the time it had been the country house of some wealthy landlord or *zamindar** from Calcutta. The whole area of three-and-a-half *bighas** had been enclosed by a brick wall then—but now there were large gaps in the wall. In the centre was a single storeyed building with three huge rooms. Once all the rooms had been illuminated by chandeliers and the central hall had had a large piano; its walls had been embellished with paintings of nude European women and in the old days the house had been popularly known as the *natchghar* or dance hall. Next to it was a medium-sized pond, its banks reinforced with brick and concrete on two sides.

Now this piece of property had become a forcibly occupied colony. Thirty-four families had staked out their territories and raised homesteads. Until a short time ago, the foundations had been of earth, the walls made from bamboo matting or tin, the roof made of tiles. One was not allowed to raise a structure on a proper

---

* For an explanation of untranslated Bengali terms, see glossary on page 205

brick foundation unless one had acquired legal rights to the land. But after having waited for so many years, those who could manage it, had raised brick buildings—some of them even dismantling the boundary wall to utilize the bricks. Only two of the families had been granted the privilege of occupying one-and-a-half rooms each of the dance hall.

Lanterns, lamps or candles were being lit in many of the houses now. The neighbourhood suffered frequent visitations from thieves—and this kind of darkness created ideal conditions for them. So the main doors of all the houses were locked. The power could remain cut off all night. It had happened before.

Sukhen and Dibya were patrolling the entire colony. It was their job at times like this—not that anybody had entrusted them with this duty. It was something they had taken upon themselves. It was natural for a person like Dibya, with his unbounded physical courage, to assure everybody of protection. Having walked all around the pond, they were approaching the clump of lychee trees, when they heard a rustling on dry leaves in the thick, sooty darkness under the branches. One could still come across an occasional snake here. When the colony had first been founded, lots of cobras and other snakes had had to be killed. In the pre-colony days, the owner and his guests would come down only two or three times a year to have a good time. So the snakes had had plenty of opportunity to multiply. The presence of so many people now had not made all of them disappear though—some tenacious ones refused to give up their holes.

In spite of Calcutta's proximity, the abundance of trees made the place look somewhat like a village. The owner of the country house had at one time planted many different kinds of trees all around his property. Seventy or so coconut trees had survived making the people of the colony self-sufficient in coconuts. Some even sold them.

Dibya tried to follow the rustling of the snake. If it happened to be one of the water snakes that often came out during the monsoon, then there was nothing to fear. He wished he had a stick or something handy to beat the pile of leaves.

Most of the colony people had picked up the Calcutta dialect by now, but they also retained their own East Bengal dialects. Among themselves, they freely mixed the two, as Dibya and Sukhen were doing now.

'Why didn't you bring your torch?' asked Dibya.

'No batteries,' said Sukhen.

'What's the point of keeping a torch if you don't have batteries?'

'Well, why don't you buy me some? You still owe me two rupees, you know.'

'Look, when I pay you back, I shall do so with interest, okay?'

Walking up to the nearest house, Dibya called out, 'Are you home, Uncle Basu?'

A thin, metallic female voice answered from within.

'No, he is not. He hasn't come home from work yet.'

'Better be careful when you step outside, a snake just passed by here.'

An East Bengali does not throw a fit at the mere mention of a snake. A dry affirmative came from the house. But two thin children rushed up to the window with eager questions.

'Dibya*da*, where did you see the snake? Where is it?'

'Never you mind. Just don't go near the pond without a light.'

The children began to feel quite excited. Everyone knew what Dibya was like. Tonight, if the lights came back, or tomorrow, he would start preparations for a snake hunt. That would be fun.

The two young men walked by Labonya's house but were disappointed at not seeing her at the window. Then they saw her grandfather and Naru.

'Where are you off to, Naru?' asked Dibya.

'To the shop.'

'What kind of fish are you having for dinner tonight?'

'No fish, we are going to have meat,' said Naru and started laughing boisterously.

'Tell your mother,' said Dibya, 'that Sukhen and I will drop in today and taste her cooking.'

'Sure,' said Grandfather Nishi heartily, 'you must

definitely come over. Naru's mother is cooking the *tree-goat* today.' *Tree-goat*, in Bengali, means the green jackfruit.

Eggplants and chillies had been planted in the little space in front of the house. The eggplants had a shining healthy look, but the chillies were not hot enough yet. A grapefruit tree had already been there from the old days. A small bamboo platform had been built underneath the tree by the settlers, and the old man spent most of his days sitting there.

*

As we know, having got hold of Naru, Grandfather Nishi had been going towards the shops, leaning on the boy's shoulder. The sudden uproar made him stop in his tracks.

'What is it, Naru?' he asked. 'Why are they shouting?'

'Oh, that's only because the lights have gone off again.'

The grandfather smiled to himself a little. Every time he heard about the lights going off, he smiled. Of course no one could see this smile in the dark—or who knows what they would have thought. This was a smile the old man enjoyed by himself. He was blind. Thirty-eight years ago, he had lost his sight completely. He had had his last look at the world even before his youth was over. Naru was his only means of locomotion.

Many people in these circumstances would think, 'What a relief if the old man died. As long as he lives he suffers himself, and makes other people suffer.'

But Labonya's family did not think that way. They all looked after the grandfather's comforts. One of the many reasons behind this was the fact that for several years now, he had been receiving a monthly stipend of seventy-five rupees from the government, as a persecuted political worker. Who would gain from his death except the government? Naru received ten paise daily from his grandfather. No other boy of his age in the colony had such an income. So he let the old man lean on his shoulder as often as was needed.

Naru's father had started a laundry in the neighbourhood. After an initial period of turmoil and uncertainty, the business seemed to have found its feet. Before the laundry, he had had a grocery shop which had been a total loss—not a single client from the colony had paid for goods they had bought on credit. The laundry was a success simply because there was no customer from the colony. It was the people from the numbered houses opposite who came to have their clothes washed. Besides, having clothes washed on credit is not considered as much a natural right as buying on credit from a grocer's!

The local *dhobis* had been contracted to wash the clothes. On rare occasions, when there was an urgent order to deliver within twenty four-hours, Labonya's mother had washed a few clothes at home for the laundry. Because of this, Labonya had sometimes been called a washerman's daughter during a quarrel. Their actual surname was Dasgupta.

The old man was in considerable pain after stumbling on the brick on the road. When you were old, even the slightest pain seemed to linger in the body. He snapped at Naru irritably.

'Damn it boy, I may be blind, but have you lost your eyes too? Why couldn't you tell me there was a brick lying here?'

'Come on grandfather, I told you about it yesterday.'

'Well, can't you remove it?'

'No, it is sunk into the earth.'

Naru's grandfather squatted down on the road himself to remove the brick. He groped about and found it, but his efforts to prise it away were futile. He obviously did not have the strength to remove obstacles in his path anymore.

Another outburst of shouting in the distance got him quickly to his feet. Naru pulled urgently at his arm.

'Quick, grandfather, do come along.'

'What is it?'

'A taxi has hit a rickshaw.'

'Where?'

'Just in front of our shop.'

'Did anyone get hurt? Who was in the rickshaw?'

'Why don't you come along quickly, so we can find out.'

'Naru, do you think anybody will beat up the taxi driver? Who is that shouting so loudly?'

The old man's hand slipped from Naru's shoulder, reducing him to a helpless flailing of limbs. The boy had run forward by himself in his excitement—but then he came running back and dragged the old man along with him. Somehow he managed to deposit his grandfather safely in their shop and rushed off to the scene of the disaster.

A taxi had grazed the wheel of a cycle-rickshaw in an attempt to avoid it. But the impact, slight as it was, had been enough to upset the rickshaw's balance and tilt it towards an open ditch close by. It had not overturned completely, of course, but one of the two lady passengers had tumbled to the ground. She had not been hurt, but her clothes were smeared with mud.

Many shadowy shapes had already gathered in the darkness. An incident like this served at least to break the monotony of the dark. Sukhen was shouting at the top of his voice and Dibya had already got a firm grip on the shoulder of the Punjabi taxi driver. The man was huge, but everyone knew quite well that at the slightest show of intransigence Dibya would split his head open. Besides, once Dibya got started, everybody else would be quite happy to assist him. Nothing could be more fun than many people beating up one person—the guilt could not be assigned to anyone in particular.

The problem with the driver was that he was aggressive—instead of being humble and apologetic, he was loudly pitching the blame on the rickshaw puller, who had refused to give way to the taxi in spite of repeated honking. But he who has been hurt cannot be the culprit. From the faceless crowd in the darkness there started building up a louder tempo of violence against the taxi driver. Dibya balled his powerful fist under the bewildered gaze of the man and spoke in ominous tones.

'Still being perverse, are you?'

At this point, the manager of the local plywood factory, another Punjabi called Kewal Singh, intervened. Coming up to Dibya, he placed a placatory hand on his shoulder.

'Why are you beating up this poor fellow, Dibu*babu*?' he asked. 'I saw him honking for dear life.'

Dibya turned towards Kewal Singh with a smile. He had become quite friendly with the man. 'Is this someone you know, Kewal Singh?'

There was a murmur in the crowd: 'These Punjabis! They always keep together. Let one turbaned head get into trouble, and the others will come rushing to his help.'

The three passengers inside the taxi continued sitting motionless. Their faces were as expressionless as concrete walls. If things started looking more dangerous, they would open the doors of the cab and melt into the crowd. That was the way things were.

Dibya smiled again at Kewal Singh. Did the man really think that he would kill this driver or what? Undue punishment for a small offence was not something Dibya cared for. Had even one of the two passengers in the rickshaw been killed, had they even broken their limbs, then, yes, then the taxi driver would have no right to live. But for a tumble into the ditch and some mud splashed on to their clothes—for this the man just had to apologize, perhaps accept a slap or two.

*

Naru's father, Biswanath, had been turning over the pages of an old receipt book with great concentration all this time. A candle burned on the table in front of him.

'Have they started fighting?' asked the grandfather. 'People seem to beat each other up for no reason these days. What's going on?'

'We don't have to know anything about it,' said Biswanath in a totally uninvolved voice. 'If the police come and ask us, we can speak the truth—that we didn't see or hear anything.'

There was always an expression of subdued grievance on Biswanath's face. He felt that too many people had cheated him. Not that he wanted to extract revenge, but he did not wish to be embroiled in the affairs of anybody either. His only aim in life was to keep his laundry business going. A number of hungry people in his home had to be provided for, and that was his main reason for living. He had not lifted his eyes once to look towards the mêlee in the darkness outside.

The candle flame trembled in the wind, and the old man kept staring at it, as if he saw the light itself—though the darkness inside him did not receive the slightest ray of light. After a short silence he spoke again. 'Haven't the lights come back on yet?'

'No.' The grandfather did not smile this time.

'Why do they have power cuts every day?' he asked anxiously. 'What are they up to?'

'Only they know anything about that.'

'Labi has her exams to take. How can she study in this darkness?'

Biswanath was jolted into further unpleasant awareness. This seemed the latest way the world wanted to ruin him. Even the electricity supply was out to get him, by cutting off the power every night. One of his sons, born just after Labonya, had died. Had he lived, he would have turned eighteen now, and perhaps been able to help his father. Labonya had failed in one subject last year. If she passed this year, she could perhaps get a teaching job in some school—and the family would have increased resources at its command. Biswanath could never think of letting his daughter work anywhere except in a school. And he did not have the money to marry her off just yet.

'Didn't they light a lantern or something at home?' he asked his father. As if the old man would know. A man who could not even sense the rising of the sun was not likely to know about lanterns.

Biswanath wanted to send Naru home immediately with some candles. The lights were not likely to come back that night, and Labonya must study. But more than one shout failed to bring any response from Naru. He was engrossed in the drama of the rickshaw and the taxi. Dibya's voice could be heard even from inside the shop.

Unable to contain her impatience at home, Labonya had finally walked out of the house. She too could hear the brawling at the end of the road, but she did not go in that direction. None of the menfolk were at home now—they had all joined the shadowy crowd in the darkness. But Labonya knew that one man would not be found there.

She stumbled at the same place where her grandfather had tripped before. She was not blind like him, but it was very dark now. She too had known about the brick, but had just been too preoccupied to notice it. In a fit of petulance, she kicked the brick again with her hurt foot, in much the same way as a little boy hits the ground on which he has fallen. Within the colony Labonya usually walked barefoot. She possessed only one pair of sandals which she wore to college.

By now, she could see quite well in the dark. She could also hear the susurration of dry leaves in motion under the lychee trees. That meant the snake was still moving about there. Labonya started stamping heavily on the ground and making loud noises to scare the snake away. No snake ever attacked human beings gratuitously.

There was no one near the pond either, one could only see the crystalline depths of dark water. In the faint moonlight, you could also see the floating water lilies at the northern edge of the pond. Often the women would come and collect them for cooking, while the lentil soup boiled on their stoves. Yet they never seemed to die out.

Labonya skirted the pond and came to one side of the dance hall. A verandah leading off the front steps and one large room had been partitioned off with a neat, woven fence. Labonya walked up the steps and called out,

'Pishima, Rangapishima!'

There was no answer. Of course, Labonya had not expected any. She knew very well that Pishima went over to the neighbouring colony this time every evening to listen to readings from the Hindu epics. Haran Thakur's rendering of the Ramayana was something that no widow in their locality could resist. But still Labonya had to call for Pishima. It was a rule of etiquette to call out the name of a senior person in the house you were visiting. Labonya took a few more steps towards the door. This time she called, 'Arjunda.'

22

But again, there was no answer. Labonya pushed the door open and entered the room, At first she could hardly make anything out. Then as her eyes grew accustomed to the darkness, she saw someone near the window, slumped forward with his head on the table. The posture somehow seemed discordantly ugly. Perhaps he was fast asleep—but it was only eight o'clock. Labonya came nearer, put a hand on his shoulder and called again, 'Arjun*da*.'

She felt something sticky on her palm and looked again, more closely, at the tall body of the young man half-lying across a table. She knew then it was blood that she had got on her palm and she screamed.

'*Jethima*, please come in here, quick. *Jethima*, Haran-*da*, *Boudi*, please—"

With the arrival of people and lights from the next room one could see the enormous wound that stretched across the head and shoulders of the young man. All over his body and scattered on the floor were congealed masses of blood. A crowbar lay on the floor. The man's old dog was to be seen moving restlessly around the room. Occasionally he would lick some blood off the floor—his master's blood. The fitful light of lanterns, a few frightened and anxious faces, the severely wounded body of an unconscious young man as it gradually slumps from the chair on to the floor, and a dog tasting blood—this is the scene before us.

II

My name is Arjun Raychoudhury. My father was the late Khitimohan Raychoudhury. My elder brother's name was Shomnath and my mother—no, one should never utter one's mother's name. A mother's name is just that, Mother. That is what we were taught in our childhood. There is a big birthmark on my right palm. Once, I found a caterpillar on my desk. I put it inside a bottle to see if it would turn into a butterfly eventually. My mother cannot switch off the lights before going to bed. She is scared to walk the distance from the switch to the bed in total darkness. I cannot stand the smell of mustard oil. Once I was nearly drowned, I was only about thirteen then and once I saved a girl from drowning. See, I remember everything.

My name is Arjun Raychoudhury. I am twenty-five years old, perhaps twenty-six. I finished my MSc exams about two-and-a-half years ago. I live in Dum Dum, in the Deshpran colony. Our house is called the dance hall. Three lizards live in my room. One of them is a really strange creature, black and white stripes all over. I smoke very little. And yet Shukla presented me with a lighter—now, where can I have kept it, where? I hope nobody is rummaging around in my desk, among my books.

H_2O is water, O_2 is oxygen, O_3 is ozone. The weight of one hydrogen atom is equal to one-sixteenth the weight of an oxygen atom; one-twelfth the weight of the carbon twelve atom is the standard... I remember everything.

I shall survive. I wasn't born to die so easily. This is a hospital bed, it is right next to the wall. I can touch it if I just stretch my arm out a little. But both my arms are pinioned with leather straps. Why have they done this to me? Have I done something wrong, committed some crime? What can be the meaning of all this? Can they imprison people in hospitals? But then, why do I think I am a prisoner? Of course, it is true that I am feeling very weak. I certainly cannot break out of these bonds.

This seems to be a huge ward. There must be at least twenty-five or thirty patients in here. I wonder if that nurse has rubber wheels fixed under her feet. Otherwise how can she walk with that silent, gliding motion, just like waves seen in a film? Which hospital is this anyway, R.G. Kar, or the Medical College Hospital?

No, I shall definitely survive. The wound is in my head, but even then it is not something to worry about. Almost everyone has to break his head some time. What I was really afraid of was that I would lose my memory. The day before yesterday, when I came to, everything seemed very hazy. I could not remember anything; even my name kept slipping away from me. But that must have been because of weakness. My name is Arjun Raychoudhury, my name is Arjun Raychoudhury. See, I remember perfectly. Even now. I can't afford to lose my memory. I have to finish writing my thesis. Besides, what on earth's the use of living like a vegetable? Oh no, I remember, remember everything.

*

'Do you remember what happened? Anything suspicious that you may have noticed, any strange people?'

'No, I can't recall anything of that sort. I was sitting by the window, when the lights suddenly went out. Somebody must have hit me from outside, perhaps they threw some heavy instrument at me—and I passed out immediately.'

'You are sure you did not see anybody?'

'Quite sure.'

'Didn't you hear anything, people talking or something like that?'

'No, nothing of that kind. But I remember hearing a

25

metallic clang, it sounded like somebody breaking a huge chain to pieces.'

'Chain?'

'Yes, it all seems like a dream. Just before I lost consciousness, I heard two things very distinctly. One, this chain-breaking sound, and then what seemed like suppressed weeping—which is impossible of course. Who could be weeping? My mother was not at home. But my dog does make these whimpering sounds at times—which could, I suppose, sound like somebody crying. But breaking a chain...'

'Oh, that's easy to explain. There wasn't any chain around. But the culprit left a crowbar behind. You must have heard that falling and striking the floor. Must say, you are really lucky to be alive.'

'Well, why should I die?'

'Nobody wants to die you know, and yet lots of people are dying every day. Anyway, I don't want to tire you out by talking. Just tell me if you suspect anyone.'

'No... I don't suspect anyone.'

'Can't you think of anybody who has a grudge against you, someone who wants settle a score with you?'

'No, I trust everybody I know. I have no reason to suspect them.'

'Haven't you had an argument with anybody in the last few days?'

'No.'

'Er, how about women?'

'What are you talking about?'

'What I mean is, young men like you often become rivals over one girl. And that can easily lead to...'

'Ha, I see what you mean. No, you can rest assured that nothing like that has ever happened.'

'Think carefully. Did your girlfriend ever become involved with another person who could have...'

'There is nothing to think about.'

'Have you recently quit one party to join another?'

'I was never a member of any party. I just didn't have the time.'

'Oh come on. Do you expect me to believe that a young man of your generation does not have time for politics?'

'I told you. I just didn't have the time.'

'Listen brother. Young people always find time to work for their parties. It is other things that they don't have the time for.'

'We had problems just in surviving. If we went in for political activities we would have starved.'

'Nonsense. Tell me the truth now. You have nothing to fear, you know. It will help us to investigate this case. These days most crimes can be traced back to inter-party clashes.'

'I have nothing more to say.'

'I'll come by again later. See if you can remember anything by then.'

*

But I do remember everything. My head still hurts, abominably, unbearably. But I do feel happiness of a kind, now that I am sure I have my memory intact. My mother must be crying her heart out. Won't they let her come and visit me? I am the only child after all. I mean now, now that my brother is dead. In a way, it is good that he is dead; if he had been alive, he would have suffered even more.

My brother used to be an extraordinarily gentle person, and very, very simple. Everyone thought he was crazy and they used to make fun of him, calling him a lunatic. That's what really drove him round the bend. He never did anybody any harm, just used to wander around by himself, sometimes talking to himself, sometimes to birds and animals—but what is wrong with that? And yet, people simply wouldn't let him remain sane. I remember one day, in front of Uncle Biswanath's laundry—no, he did not have a laundry then, it was his grocery store—a group of boys tormenting my poor brother. They surrounded him and pulled all his clothes off—I couldn't check my tears at the sight of him, so pitiful, so helpless. But I could do nothing. Children can be so hard to control, even their elders were standing around grinning, instead of trying to stop them. Of course it is hard to stop children when they get carried away by the exhilaration of a particularly cruel sport. And one can be terribly cruel in childhood. Didn't I myself find pleasure in pulling the wings off dragonflies?

My mother used to weep for my brother. After all, what else does a poor widow have but her tears? And when my brother really went mad, I could do nothing to provide for his treatment. Only rich people should lose their sanity, for it is an expensive disease. And I—I was getting a monthly scholarship of thirty rupees in those days, plus another eighty from tutoring two students. My brother always made a fuss if there was no fish with his rice; and yet how often could I get fish for him? Not to speak of proper medicines. My poor mother did her best of course. Herbal medicines, charms, amulets—nothing was left untried. Towards the end, my brother would keep saying to me, 'Let's go back home. Don't you know, India and Pakistan have become one country again? Gandhi has fixed everything, he's managed to patch up all our differences.'

Gandhi had been assassinated fourteen years ago. I can still see that scene vividly. My brother standing before me, his face half-hidden by a beard, his hair matted and tangled from not having bathed for days, his eyes glittering. There was a rolled up newspaper in his hand and he was shouting at me with intense faith. 'Arjun, how can you not have seen this? Look, it's in the headlines here, that India and Pakistan have been re-united. Gandhi has done it all—he's even made Jinnah and Nehru embrace each other. Do let's go back home. Let's not stay in this horrible place any longer.'

Strange that it should have been the same paper he was showing me, that carried headlines about the communal riots.

Yes, I am really a selfish person. Even now, whenever I think of my brother it is fear I feel more than sorrow. Doesn't insanity tend to run in the family? Grandfather Nishi says that my father wasn't quite normal either. In his youth he would often go away from home for three or four months at a time. And when he came back, you couldn't get a word out of him as to what he'd been doing. We came to know later that he had a tendency to seek out all the holy men or *sadhus* that he heard of. He felt he had something to find out from him. In the end, of course, he had to give up this search. The tentacles of the family and of various attachments had imprisoned him. But the knowledge of his past had left this core of fear in me—would I too show signs of abnormality, would I too go insane? For what then would become of my mother? Especially with the kind of head injury that I have now—but no, nothing has happened to my mind. I remember everything perfectly.

*

'Who is it? Oh, it is you Shukla. When did you come in? How did you get to hear about me? In the newspaper? Surely not. I can't imagine the papers wanting to write about me. I am not even involved in politics. Have you come with your brother? Oh, of course, you couldn't have. He is giving a seminar in Allahabad, isn't he? So who did you come with?'

'Arju*nda*, do you recognize me?'

'Recognize you? Sure I do. Why shouldn't I?'

'Well go on, tell me who I am.'

'You are Shukla. Why do you ask me these silly questions'

'Okay, I won't ask them again. Do please keep quiet though. The doctors say you shouldn't speak at all. Why, what are you doing? You mustn't try to get up. No, I insist, you must lie still, absolutely still.'

'All right then, tell me who you came with.'

'Why do you keep asking that over and over again? Can't I have come by myself?'

'You can, I'm sure. But I have never seen you go anywhere alone before.'

'How do you feel?'

'I think I am almost well by now. But tell me, do you know why they have tied my arms down?'

'Because you kept trying to scratch your head all the time you were running a temperature.'

'Of all the stupid things to do. How can they expect me not to scratch myself when I feel like it?'

29

'It's dangerous to touch that wound. It can become infected. Besides...'

'But Shukla, you have no idea how uncomfortable it is, if your head is itching all over and you can't scratch it. One feels as if nothing else in the world matters. As if one could give anything just for the privilege of scratching oneself. Please, Shukla dear, do tell them to untie my arms for a while.'

'Why on earth should they listen to me?'

'Of course they will. Your father is such a well-known doctor. He must carry a lot of weight round here. And many of the doctors here probably know you well too. Otherwise they wouldn't have let you visit me now, would they, when it's not visiting hours? Do be an angel, and tell them.'

'But I can't possibly ask them to do something like that!'

'Well then, since there aren't any nurses around now, why don't you untie my bandage and scratch my head a little?'

'I can't do that. Shall I try scratching from the top?'

'How can you scratch me over the bandage? It's no good, unless you actually touch the skin.'

'Well, let me just stroke your head then.'

'I can't feel a thing. Why have they covered up my whole head like this? I can't feel your touch.'

'Do you know how many stitches the doctors had to put in? Eleven! It's a wonder you are still alive.'

'There you go again. Why shouldn't I be alive? It's not that easy to die.'

'You are talking too much. I have to go now.'

'Please don't. Stay just a little bit longer. You didn't come with anybody else, did you? Or have Probal or Akhtar come with you? I suppose they must have. You never go anywhere alone. What a piece of luck really, breaking my head like this. Otherwise I wouldn't have had you sitting with me for such a long time. One can never get you alone. And yet, the trouble is, now that I do have you to myself, I can't think of things to say. I am not much good at thinking up nice things to say, you know...'

'Well who wants you to make pretty speeches? Can't

you just lie there quietly?'

'But Shukla, I know that there's something important I want to say to you. Only, I can't think of a way to say it.'

'That's all right. You can lie here and think about it. I'll come by again tomorrow and you can tell me then. I have to go now.'

'No, please, stay a little longer. It is so tedious to have to lie in bed day after day.'

'But look Arjun*da*, the nurse is coming this way now. And she had given me permission to stay with you for five minutes only.'

'You smell lovely. It must be a very expensive perfume. Was it a gift from someone?'

'Of course, it was. Can't you guess who?'

'Akhtar or Barun. Could even be Ranajoy. Not Probal, I think. Who was it?'

'I won't tell you.'

'Whoever it was, you did well to wear it. In a hospital it makes you feel really good to smell such nice perfume. Actually, I think the nurses should also wear good perfume. That would cheer up the patients every time they came close to them. But all you get here is the smell of antiseptics, night and day.'

'I really must go now, Arjun*da*. And listen, your mother's all right, you know. I asked after her.'

'Stay a little more, do please. Let me inhale your perfume some more.'

'Come on Arjun*da*, don't be so childish now. I've never seen you act this way before.'

'Yes, but I am a sick person now. People regress into childhood when they are in a hospital. Have you ever been in one?'

'Only once, at birth.'

'Right, that's why you have not been silly and childish ever since you were born. You are much too intelligent and cruel.'

'That's enough. The nurse will come and scream at me any minute. I must go.'

'Aren't you going to scratch my head a little?'

'No, you have bugs crawling inside that head of yours. Plain scratching won't do you any good.'

31

If only I had got to know Shukla and her brother Abanish earlier, I might have been able to do something for my brother. Abanish*da's* father is a very well-known doctor. I'm sure he would have made some arrangements for my brother if I had requested him. But I was in my first year at college when my brother died. And I only met Abanish*da* when I got to the university. He was one of our professors, and even now he is an adviser on my research. Knowing how poor I was, he found two students for me to tutor. He also asked me to tutor his sister, but Shukla refused. Nothing, she declared, would induce her to take tutelage from such a juvenile instructor. Just as well, of course. I don't think I could have felt easy with Abanish*da* and his family, if I had had a financial arrangement with them.

But my poor brother, I just keep thinking about him. When I first gained consciousness at the hospital, and felt that my mind was a blank, I was really scared that I had lost my memory. What if I had become like him? He went mad slowly, in front of my eyes. He was such a simple fellow, my brother, with occasional whims. So often have I seen him sitting on the balcony, absorbed in watching the comings and goings of ants. And as for the *shalik* birds, he had frequent conversations with them. The dog, of course, was his constant companion. Can one really call this insanity? The big pond in our colony had hardly any fish left in it. But my brother would sit there for hours, holding his line with infinite patience in the hot summer sun. There used to be a white stork too, near the pond, which stood on one leg with a patience matching my brother's. I had been a good marksman from childhood. I could throw stones accurately at trees in order to get the fruits. I even made a bow and arrow out of pieces of split bamboo, and riddled the banana trees with holes. And once, it so happened, I killed that stork with a slingshot. My brother was very upset about it. For quite a few days he moped around, as if he had lost an old friend. He didn't scold me though. He never said a word in anger to anyone.

Dibya, I remember, once hit him. Of course, Dibya has always been particularly headstrong and perverse. Why else would anyone want to beat up a simple, inoffensive fellow like my brother? The poor fellow never got involved in the doings of others, nor did he ever hurt anyone's feelings. But Dibya had been convinced that he was only pretending to be abnormal, so that he would not have to do any work. A good thrashing, Dibya had seemed to think, was the best cure for that kind of malingering madness. But, as I have said before, my brother was not really a raving lunatic. He was only a bit simple, slightly whimsical, and very, very harmless. Most people cannot understand this sort of person. They think everybody should be violently and acutely motivated by self interest. Whoever deviates from this norm, must be mad. So they really drove him mad with a vengeance. They forced him to take a job at the Ghughudanga factory. But how could my poor brother possibly work as a factory labourer? The forcible transition from open fields and wide-flowing rivers to this dingy urban life had been bad enough for him. I would go and attend classes in college, but all the time I would keep seeing the same picture in front of my eyes—my brother wandering about the streets in tattered clothes and dragging the dog along with him, while the boys ran after him, throwing stones.

No, I haven't lost my memory the way he did. I remember—only too well.

A raised path between fields, paddy on one side and jute on the other. Small canals had been dug through the fields and almost met the path. Cane grew on the banks. We boys would go there to eat the ripe cane fruit. One particular cane bush had a couple of crested bulbuls nesting in it—the kind we called the foreign bulbuls. I remember once bringing home a couple of bluish bulbul eggs in the vain hope of hatching them. I wonder if the bulbuls still nest in that cane bush.

I left my country at the age of eleven. Yes, my country. I cannot remember the time of partition very well. But my earliest memories do go back to an awareness of belonging to Pakistan. My father's generation spent time lamenting the glories of the past. But I never saw the slightest sign of any such glory. All I could see was us boys being constantly warned—against going too far alone, against having any kind of fight with the Muslim boys at school. School was three miles from home, a daily walk for us. But the monsoon submerged everything in water. Boats were the only answer then. We could not afford our own boat. So I would start early from home and wait under the big banyan tree by the river—in case a boat happened by and could ferry me over. Some days, of course, there would be no boats. Then the only thing to do was to undress behind the banyan tree, wrap your books up in your clothes, hold the bundle over your head with one hand, and swim across. Abanishda was convulsed with laughter when he heard this story. Later he asked me, 'But weren't you ashamed to take your clothes off in public like that, a big boy of eleven?'

Certainly not. What was there to be ashamed of? Once I got to the other side, I would stand for a few minutes drying myself in the sun. Many people must have seen me then. Going to school used to be an addiction for me. Shukla once asked me, 'How could you swim such a long distance when you were only a boy? Who taught you to swim?' What a silly thing to ask! As if somebody had to teach East Bengali boys to swim. In a country of rivers the humans learned to swim from childhood, as effortlessly as the waterbugs.

No, shame came to me in Calcutta, at the age of seventeen. Usually I never went out of the house on the morning of Holi. But on that particular occasion, ·I remember having to go out in the afternoon. A group of non-Bengalis drenched me with their coloured dyes. At that time I possessed only that one shirt, and I had nothing else to wear to college the next day. My brother had by then become quite unbalanced, and wandered about the streets. My mother shed tears in her sad solitude at not being able to give us two meals a day. So there was never any question of buying another shirt for myself. And I was stubborn too. I went along to Presidency College wearing that multicoloured shirt. But I could not bear the derisive smirks of my fellow students—tears of rage and shame blurred my sight.

34

Haranda later took pity on me and gave me an old shirt of his the next day.

I was always the top of my class in the village school. Many of the boys were both resentful and envious of me because of this. But, really, I never felt I was a hero simply because I could outstrip the others in school work. My father had taken my brother out of school because he had failed twice in Class VIII. This was the fear that spurred me on. I worked frantically for fear of being made to leave school, and succeeded in learning all our lessons by heart. Besides, as we were perpetually poor, we couldn't ever manage to pay our way through any school or college. So I had to do well enough to get free schooling all along. Up to Class III, I used to go to the Board School, which was free anyway. And in high school, I got a free studentship, because I was the first boy in my class. Indeed, it became a habit with me, coming first in class.

The headmaster of our school was a man called Amjad Ali. He was well-known and respected throughout the whole sub-division. I was one of his favourites. But his son, Yaqub, hated me with a passion. He was a couple of years older, and frequently found reasons to beat me up. But I could never understand the reason for such hatred.

I remember having two possessions which were extremely precious to me. One was a red and blue pencil and the other a silver harmonica. The pencil was red at one end and blue at the other. In the obscure village where I lived, such things were rare indeed. Conscious that it would be short-lived, I seldom used the pencil— only to underline the very important passages in my textbooks. As for the harmonica, nobody was ever allowed to touch it but myself. I feel so ashamed now to think that I did not even allow my brother to play it. A neighbour of ours, who had become an uncle by adoption, used to work in the navy. He would come home every two years, and bring back marvellous gifts. We used to call him Navy Uncle. The harmonica and the pencil were both brought back by him. Both carried the inscription, 'Made in Germany', and they had been bought in Germany too.

Looking back now, I can see that I really was a spoilt little brat, the kind that is favoured by the teachers in school and pampered by family and neighbours. The boys in my class sometimes sneered at me because of this. But what could I have done? The elders would never scold me even if I had been up to mischief. Some other unfortunate boy was usually punished. All my good results in class won me this total indulgence. But I really could not help it, you know. A couple of careful readings and everything would be imprinted on my brain. I had no option but to be top of my class.

We were poor when we lived in the village. But our mother never let her two boys feel any deprivation. The neighours too did their best to help us. Often they would invite my brother and myself over for delectable meals. All this attention resulted in my becoming extraordinarily thin-skinned. If, by chance, anybody did speak roughly to me, I would be absolutely crushed.

Our uncle in the navy would always bring back nice presents whenever he came home. But I only remember the pencil and harmonica.

I was returning home from school one day, when the pencil fell out of my hand. Yaqub picked it up and said, 'Let me have this pencil.'

I tried to snatch it away from him, saying, 'No, no...' But Yaqub raised his hand out of my reach and said, 'If you won't give it to me, I won't let you have it either.'

He was stronger than I. I simply could not manage to get it away from him. He was laughing as he walked away from me. I told my father about it when I reached home. But he did not give it much importance.

'It's only a pencil after all. Why can't he have it?'

I complained bitterly to all our neighbours. But everybody came up with the same response, that I should keep quiet about it instead of making a big thing of it. Amjad Ali was not only the headmaster of the school, he was also the President of the Union Board. People somehow took it for granted that his son could behave like a thug whenever he wished to. After all, in the old days, nobody had had the nerve to stand up to the sons of the *zamindars* and the landlords. Who would have dreamt of denying them something that they demanded? People like Amjad Ali and his family were present-day landlords. All our relatives and neighbours would look at one another with sad regret and say, 'Only ten years ago, they wouldn't even dare look us straight in the eye when speaking to us. But just look at the way things are now! This is the kind of independence Gandhi has brought us. To be the slaves of fear in our own land!'

My father glanced at my face, still hurting with resentment, and said, 'Never mind son. Forget about that pencil. I'll get you another.' False consolation, as it happened. He was never able to buy me another red and blue pencil.

Children have an intense and direct sense of right and wrong. Adults often pretend not to notice a violation of what is right just as often as they are unable to recognize what is right. My elders did not attach any importance to my sorrow over losing that pencil, but I could never forget it. I found it perfectly understandable that in itself, one boy taking away a bit of pencil from another in school would not seem anything but trivial to an adult. But in my case, they were definitely perturbed enough to discuss it at length. And yet, they never did anything to retrieve that pencil. That meant that the taking away of a pencil symbolized many other kinds of deprivation to them. But I was not to realize those implications at that age. All that I experienced was the frequent tearfulness of hurt, bewilderment and the ever-present sense of loss because of the red and blue pencil, so evocative of strange, mysterious lands.

In many other ways, my childhood was rather a deprived one. There was a man who used to sell long, stick-like candy in front of our school. I never had the money to buy one. The Laskar boys used to make a point of showing their candy to me when they ate it. Yaqub, Bashir and some other boys used to play with Royal brand marbles. I never managed to buy one. My brother used to get a kind of grapefruit as a ball for me to play with. Showkat's uncle once bought him a green T-shirt with a zipper from Dacca. He looked really good in it. But I had to wear unfashionable shirts sewn at home by my mother. I had only two valuable possessions—the harmonica and that red and blue pencil. Why should Yaqub get hold of those?

I don't know to how many people I told my story of woe—but no one bothered to do anything. One day the headmaster happened to be taking our English class. I was sitting there, despondent. Whenever he took our classes, I was the last one asked to answer a question. I was only asked when everybody else had failed to answer. That day it was the spelling of the word rhinoceros that had stymied the boys. The headmaster looked at me and said, 'Come Arjun, you must tell them what it is.'

I hunched my shoulders, and said, 'I don't know.'

Every boy in class knew as well as the headmaster that the word was nothing to me. Why, I never made a mistake even in spelling words like conscience or hygiene. The headmaster stared at me in amazement.

'Can't spell this word. Why don't you try?'

'No, I won't.'

He walked up to me, pushed my chin up with one finger and said sternly, 'Why? Why won't you answer me?'

Normally we were petrified of the headmaster. Whenever he was angry the victim would receive a caning. But at that particular moment, I felt no fear. The desperation born of childish hurt is desperate indeed. Everybody at home had warned me not to breath a single word about that pencil. But I could not help saying in a heated voice, 'Why should Yaqub take away my pencil?'

Emotion slurred my words, and the whole question was so irrelevant, that the headmaster at first had trouble understanding me. He frowned at me and asked, 'Pencil? What pencil are you talking about?'

Jagannath, who sat next to me, had been pulling at my shirt all the time to stop me from saying any more. Yaqub, after all, was feared by everybody. But I just went ahead, saying, 'I am not going to study in this school anymore.'

'Why not?' asked the headmaster.

'Yaqub has taken my pencil.'

Amjad Ali brooded in silence for a while over that one. Then he called Yaqub over to the blackboard. Yaqub stood there, looking at me with an evil, red gleam in his eyes. In front of a roomful of boys, Amjad Ali announced, 'This boy is not only a thief but a liar. He lied to me at home. It is more of a sin to lie than to steal. He should be punished. Arjun, you come up here and box his ears.'

Boxing Yaqub's ears was not something I particularly cared for. All I wanted was to have my pencil back. But Amjad Ali forced me to do it—I somehow made myself just touch Yaqub's ears. But the consequences of this act were to make things more difficult. The whole village hummed with the news. In 1955 it was a terrible matter for a Hindu boy to box the ears of a Muslim boy. For several days our family quaked with fear.

Mr. Amjad Ali is a person whom I remember very well. There was another thing he said some other day, which I have not forgotten. It was sometime after the pencil incident. Amjad Ali happened to be the kind of person who deplored the stupidity of the insane rage building up between the two countries (India and Pakistan). It is true that a faulty social system had allowed the Hindus to exploit the Muslims of East Bengal (now Bangladesh). But Amjad Ali clearly said he was not in favour of making the helpless people of a later age pay the price of that oppression. Political ignorance and obstinacy had led to the splitting of one country into two, each of which had one religion as its majority. But to oppress the minority in any country seemed churlish to him. However, in those days of feverish lunacy, people like him did not command popular attention.

Later, of course, the people of East Bengal changed a lot. They realized that you could not rule a country in the name of religion. People of the same religion could exploit each other just as much, fight as bitterly over the conflict of interests. And when that realization came, it was people like Amjad Ali who stepped forward to reconstruct East Bengal. But in 1954 or 1955, the prevalent atmosphere was not so healthy. Heavy pressure was being exerted to make an Islamic military state

39

out of East Bengal. And people like Amjad Ali belonged to a very small, sane minority.

After that last incident in school, I was walking home one day when Yaqub, along with four or five other boys, waylaid me and took away my pencil, my harmonica and my books. They also told me that if I reported this to Amjad Ali again, then my parents would find my body in the jute fields. All those boys boxed my ears so hard that they turned red. They also took care to inform me that it was a great pleasure for them to treat a Brahmin's son in this fashion. Then they knocked me down and went off, one of them playing my harmonica.

The enclave where our house was, used to be called *Puranbari* (literally, 'old house')—a neighbourhood consisting of seven or eight families. When all the elders of *Puranbari* heard of this incident, they decided that I was not to be sent to school for a month. They also told me never to talk about this to anybody. It is quite easy to force a little boy of eleven to stay at home. Amjad Ali was considered a decent person. But one of his brothers was a big shot in the Muslim League. Everybody in the village went in terror of him. And at that time, the Muslim League had tremendous power in East Bengal. That was the party which had brought about Pakistan— naturally enough, their word was law. It was hard to find any man there, Hindu or Muslim, who was not scared of the bigwigs in the party. Our community members had been so overcome with terror, that they did not even have the guts to ask for fair play.

The partition of India meant many losses for many people. Some lost their lives, some everything they possessed. So if I say that I lost my pencil and that harmonica, it can sound surprisingly inconsequential. But you see, those were my only cherished possessions. Along with them, I lost the red and blue and silver dreams of my childhood. All the private places where I used to play my harmonica—beside the pond, in the bamboo groves, next to the cane bushes—all these places later bore witness to outbursts of weeping.

I had never seen a riot in my village. Riots never do happen in villages, they are usually entirely urban happenings. For in a village everyone knows everyone else. After all, it is difficult to kill a person you know. So on the whole, we had had an amicable relationship with the Muslims in our village. Apart from the Muslims, there was a substantial number of untouchables in our village too. At one time it was forbidden for us caste Hindus to set foot in their enclave. When untouchable persons came to our house, they would stand outside in the courtyard and talk. If they even happened to lean against the wall, we would have to throw away our drinking water; the slightest bodily contact with them meant a change of clothes. And yet, now, we were desperately trying to establish a common identity of Hindu-ness with them, so that they could swell our ranks. The village elders started treating them with deference. Any time an incident of terror was reported, these old men would whisper among themselves, 'The untouchables will side with us, they have to side with us.'

But though we had never had to witness a riot in our own village, we could not avoid hearing about riots in nearby Narayanganj, or even Dacca. And every time that happened, a pall of fear would descend on us. The ultimate terror was to hear of a riot in India. And it was this terror that was so unbearable. Day and night there was only one apprehensive expectation—when will it come, when will somebody attack us? On such days, even the boys would stop playing, the women wouldn't quarrel with one another, the old men would not gossip about other people—a lowering cloud would settle on each and every face. Occasionally, I still see that phenomenon today. If there is a communal riot in Gujarat, the faces of the Muslim population in Calcutta bear the mark of anxiety. After all, it takes only one madman to light a fire, the flames of which can spread ravenously in untold directions.

The Muslims in our village, who had had an education, often commented in front of us that there were many more incidents of riots in Hindustan (India) than in Pakistan, even though Hindustan prided itself on being a secular state. True, there was no way of refuting this. But inwardly we would ask, whose fault is it? Who stands

41

to gain by provoking such riots? In those days, nobody in Pakistan used the names Bharat or India. It was always Hindustan. Yet no country called Hindustan exists any more on the map of the world.

However, though we did not have riots in the village, burglaries and hold-ups were steadily on the increase. Not just at night either, but during the day as well. It was never any use to go to the police. If the person you suspected of theft, or even had seen committing the crime, happened to be a Muslim, you could never mention his name. For then the officer in charge of the police station would loudly declare it to be an attempt to vilify the Muslims. If we were so scared of crimes, then why didn't we go to Hindustan? Nobody was forcing us to stay. By that time, many non-Bengali Muslims from Bihar and the other western states of India had migrated to East Bengal. It was mostly they who were given jobs as guards and policemen, and their hatred of the Hindus was extreme.

Gradually we started noticing how one Hindu house after another became empty. Those among us who were relatively better off, or those who had relatives in India, would just pack up and leave for India. Their preparations were so secret that not even their neighbours would get wind of it. Any land they possessed, they would sell at ridiculous prices. Homesteads were left unsold, for sentimental reasons.

I remember the Banerji house—a huge magnificent mansion. The only concrete building in our village, three storeys high. An iron gate in front. Now, that house is surrounded by encroaching weeds and bushes, the lair of jackals and civet cats. These cats, which were small replicas of tigers, would sit in the wilderness at night and scream. We children would often playfully shout at them, 'Cheap or dear'. The response sounded an approximation of "dear" so we felt that even those wretched animals could foretell the coming inflation.

In my limited childhood experience, the Banerji mansion symbolized the ultimate expression of wealth and magnificence. And everyone referred to it as the Banerji House. Ganapati Banerji's handsome, educated sons held jobs in different places—Calcutta, Bombay, even London. But the elderly Ganapati had stayed on in East Bengal with all his other relatives, dependents and hangers-on. He had a rifle with which he fired blanks, anytime there was a furore in the village. And what a variety of fruit grew in their orchard—different kinds of mangoes, lychees, seven or eight types of guava and countless others. We would stand outside the gates and gaze at them. For we were forbidden to enter. One night, a few of us did dare to sneak in, but the huge dogs gave us the chase of our lives.

So nobody had a clue as to why the powerful Banerjis eventually had to leave the village. The story went that the District Magistrate had insulted Ganapati Banerji, and hurt his feelings irrevocably. After all, ever since the days of the British Raj, magistrates, sub-divisional officers and superintendents of police had stayed at the Banerji House whenever they came to the village. And the one or two days of their stay was always made into an important occasion. The very best food would be procured for them. It was considered a great honour to be able to house the magistrate or superintendent of police. And many of them had accepted the hospitality of the Banerjis. But now, a magistrate could summon Ganapati Banerji to his court and insult him in public!

I do not know how much of their land the Banerjis managed to sell. But the house was not disposed of. All the furniture—even the iron gates and doors and windows—was left behind for the taking, and those disappeared soon enough. Inexorably, the wilderness took over, so that even in broad daylight the sight of the house made you shiver. Rumour had it that Ganapati Banerji's father's ghost had come to haunt the house he himself had built. He could be seen wandering about the place every evening.

My brother and I did enter the house one afternoon. It had been his idea.

'Come let's go and get some mangoes,' he had said to me.

As we went, I remembered an incident which had happened when I was much younger. The Banerjis were celebrating a religious festival with extraordinary splendour. Lights in the garden, decorations of flowers and paper chains. Relatives from different places had come for the occasion. How beautiful their clothes were! And the women—fair-skinned and beautiful like the images of goddesses, the sound of their laughter like sweet unfamiliar music. I stood outside those iron gates with my face pressing against the bars and looked and looked. I can still see myself as I was then, bare-bodied, a thin boy dressed only in a pair of shorts, gazing wide-eyed on a fairy-tale world where there was only happiness and plenty. Then my father came up behind me, put a hand on my shoulder and said, 'What are you doing here? You should not stand here like this, son. They'll think you are a beggar boy.'

My brother and I wandered around the deserted, desolate house for a long time. Occasionally my flesh would creep, for I thought I could hear deep sighs. My brother went on picking up derelict objects—a broken pair of glasses, an empty jar of face cream. He looked as if he was expecting to stumble on hidden treasure any minute. Then we came to a huge mango tree. The fruit was longish in shape, parrot green in colour. Sweet as honey too. Thick jungle growth surrounded the tree. But when we came close, we saw four or five people squatting on the ground, engaged in some secret activity. We were immediately terrified. One of them was Rajjab Sheikh. He glared at us and said, 'Look at these Brahmin brats, snooping around here. Get lost.'

We seemed to be getting more than our fair share of insults just because we were Brahmins.

After the Banerjis, it was the Duttas' turn to leave. The family used to have quite a prosperous grocery store in the main market. They also owned extensive agricultural land. Their house was next to the canal; on the other side lived the Muslim peasants. I remember that year there were a lot of dying fish floating on the surface of the canal. We knew that if you put carbolic soap in the pond, the fish would die. Enemies often did that to you. But why on earth should fish be dying off in the canal? Many people thought that the fish had been poisoned, and one should not eat them. But the poor cannot afford the luxury of being finicky over such things. The poor don't die that easily anyway.

So we spent one whole morning and afternoon splashing around in the waters of the canal. One by one, the fish kept on floating up to the surface, very weak, sometimes turning up on their stomachs. But they were hard to get hold of. As soon as we touched them, they would slip out and surface again further off. But eventually I did manage to get a five-pound carp. And as for my brother, he really caught quite a few, of different kinds. In the end, he even got a fishbone stuck in his hand.

All this fishing made us very tired. So we went over to the Dutta house, to ask for a drink of water. The servant, Purandar, brought us water in a shining bell metal jug. But when the old grandmother noticed it, she told him off very sharply. Apparently, one should never give children water by itself. It is supposed to bring bad luck to the house. So she sent Amala*di* to us with some pressed coconut sweets. I'll never forget the magic of that taste. After that, we boys used to turn up at that house with or without reason, just to drink some water. Every time Amala*di* would give us those same sweets. So we started referring to the house among ourselves as 'the sweet house'.

Mr. Dutta had four daughters; no sons, not even sons-in-law. Amala*di* had been widowed two years after her wedding and had come back to her father's home. She had a very quiet and serene nature; her face was like the still, quiet waters of a pond in the afternoon. Nobody had ever heard her raise her voice. If there was a severe illness in any house, Amala*di* would be summoned to nurse the patient. Efforts were being made at that time to find a husband for the next sister, Kamala*di*. In those days, it was becoming increasingly difficult to find eligible bridegrooms for Hindu girls in Pakistan.

There are some women who show strong maternal tendencies, even from their childhood. They are born to be mothers, in motherhood lies their happiness. When we saw Amala*di* she was only twenty-two or twenty-three.

45

But she never behaved with us like an elder sister, she was more like a mother. And yet, she had been widowed at twenty, so her promise of maternity was doomed to remain unfulfilled. That was why she always made a point of feeding the little boys in the village, whenever she saw them. While we ate, she would look at us with deep, lingering tenderness. Seven-year-old Abbas from the fishermen's community had lost his mother. He would spend practically all his time with Amaladi.

I still remember there was not a breath of scandal about Amaladi. It is fairly easy to spread ugly gossip about a healthy young widow. But whenever we went near Amaladi, we seemed to sense an emanation of purity, somewhat like the haloes painted around the heads of gods and goddesses. And she was always so concerned about our well-being—which one of us had got up from the sickbed, which one had lost weight, nothing went unnoticed.

Amaladi had not had much education. Often she would say to me, 'Arjun, you'd better work hard in school. Then you will have to come and tell me all about the many strange countries of the world.' Though Amaladi was a widow, she still managed to remind me of the picture of a woman saint in my school-books.

I am sure she understood quite well why we went to her house so often to ask for a drink of water. But she never showed an unwelcoming face. The amazing thing was that the sweets were always prepared in that house. Every day. We never had to have water by itself. Amaladi would just look at us, and say, 'Come and sit down children. You must be thirsty. Have a bit of a sweet first.' And those wonderful sweets, made of thickened milk and coconut, redolent of camphor. The taste still lingers in my mouth.

Altaf, the postmaster's son, was a great friend of mine. He and I spent quite a few afternoons talking to Amaladi. We were about ten, but she never made us feel unimportant because of our age.

Her younger sister, Kamaladi, was a more aggressive person. She once told me off very sharply because we had taken a lime from one of their trees, the kind of lime that has a strong fragrance. But Amala*di* happened to come by and said, 'How can you scold them like that just for picking one lime? How can you? That tree is loaded with limes. What can we possibly do with all of them?' Then she herself picked some limes and stuffed them into our pockets, Altaf's and mine.

I don't know why I suddenly thought of Amala*di* today. It would have been better not to.

The jute fields stretched over several miles, the plants as high as a man, some even higher. I have never seen such jute fields anywhere in West Bengal. We boys used to play quite often in those wide, green fields of jute. Not only was it easy for us children to hide there, but even grown men could disappear from sight if they sat down among the jute plants. If you chased thieves, they would inevitably make for the jute fields to escape. It was in one of those fields that a group of boys discovered Amala*di*'s body. I wasn't there with them, but my brother was. Her throat had been cut, there were innumerable stab wounds all over her body, and not a shred of clothing on her. After ravishing her they could not be content with just killing her, they had wanted to hack her to pieces.

There are some people in this world who cannot bear the existence of anything beautiful. Beauty for them is inevitably for destruction. In those days there was nothing I could imagine that was more beautiful than Amala*di*.

Perhaps it is because I was not an actual witness to the discovery in the jute fields, that it brings such horror to my mind. I still can't get over it. Everybody in the village shed tears for Amala*di*. My brother came running home from the jute fields and passed out as soon as he set foot in our courtyard. That was when he started having those occasional fainting spells. Dear Amala*di*, I have read many books, learnt many things now, but it is too late to tell you any stories.

Fifteen days after this, the Duttas left East Bengal. A group of Bihari refugees had come and settled in Madaripur. Sometimes they would come into our village and glare at us with the red lust of blood in their eyes.

Everyone blamed them secretly for this incident. Not that our police did anything about it. Mr. Dutta took his wife and daughters away with him. But his parents, the old grandmother and grandfather, stayed on. The old people wanted to die in their ancestral home. Sometimes, when I went down to the canal, I would see grandfather watering his vegetable plots, and grandmother sitting on the porch, waiting with empty eyes for the advent of death. Whenever I saw them, I felt my mouth going dry. But I never went into that house again to ask for a drink of water.

And so it went. One by one, the Sarkars, the Mitras, the Rays—all left the village. Like pawns being removed from a chessboard. But we were very poor, we had no other place to go to.

My father still believed that India and Pakistan would become one again. All those who had left the village would return, and everything would be splendidly complete again. Relatives and family members working in faraway places like Calcutta, Delhi or Bombay would come home for the annual Puja festival. Muslim friends and peasants would also come, invited to the Puja feast. The drums and cymbals would once again deafen the ears as the devotional ritual of the *arati* was carried out. My father went around declaring, 'The saint Arabindo has said that we don't have to wait much longer. Unity will come by 1957. Hindus and Muslims will embrace each other as brothers, and the past will be past. In the future, we shall remain brothers.' My father was a teacher in the government school. He had the habit of lapsing into English phrases quite frequently. I still remember, his monthly salary was thirty-two rupees, and even that was not paid regularly.

When the first wave of the exodus took place, many of the elder Muslims in the village came to us and expressed their regrets. Some of them we called brother or uncle. They would say, 'Why do you all have to leave? We have no bitterness between ourselves. We will stay together in friendship and harmony. And as long as we are around, we won't allow anybody to lay a finger on you. But if you let yourselves be terrorized into leaving, then those bastards will only entrench themselves even more firmly.' And some of these old men shed tears as they spoke.

But the problem was that it was never possible to identify 'those bastards'. On the whole, we had been on amicable terms with the Muslims in our village. Occasionally, one or two people would glare at us or ridicule us. But by and large, the innocence of ordinary villagers resists mutation. Even among the boys in my school there was not much antagonism. True, I had had a problem with the Head's son, but that could happen anywhere. And my brother had many Muslim friends. Whenever I went to Altaf's house, his family always received me with affection.

Yet there was a creeping awareness of fear among us, as if we were criminals of some sort. If we received injustice, we accepted it without expecting redress. Our position was like that of a servant suspected of theft. Even if he is innocent, he has no way of asserting that. He has to submit to being beaten up, and often has to lose his job. The misconceptions of a few ignorant leaders turned millions of people into servants. I wonder how much of this extraordinary irresponsibility will be recorded in history.

Not that I myself was old enough to grasp the implications of all this at that time. But later I realized that even after the creation of Pakistan, the Muslims of East Bengal continued to be deprived; the promise of happiness and prosperity was not realized. It is true that once the competition with the Hindus was eradicated, Bengali Muslims had a greater chance to receive education, they had access to many more jobs, and slowly there was the emergence of a middle class among them. But they still remained the victims of economic exploitation at the hands of the West Pakistanis. The Bengali Muslims never managed to acquire power; the West Pakistanis continued to play the part of foreign overlords. So in absolute terms, it would not be a mistake to say that within the framework of Pakistan, East Bengal never achieved freedom. Two fragments of land with a thousand sundering miles between them—the only connecting link being Islam. It took them a long time to realize how absurd the link was. The holders of power in Pakistan had no proper adherence to Islam. In their manner, life-style, food and habits, they aped the British. Islam was only used by them as a peg on which to hang their anti-India dogmas or their hatred of Hindus.

When the Hindus in East Bengal stopped selling their land, the situation changed even more. Even ordinary villagers started feeling greedy. For if the Hindus could be frightened into leaving without selling their property, then their land could be taken possession of. Most of the Muslim peasants were extremely poor; they had hardly ever had a good meal. How long could you expect them to suppress the desire to acquire free land? It was not their fault—the fault lay with those who had created the reason for such needs. Non-Bengali Muslims also tried to fan the flame of this greed. I don't know much about the people in the cities who had political interests. But this I can say, that I had never before seen antagonism between ordinary villagers on the grounds of religion. It was the non-Bengali outsiders who came in and tried to foment disputes and disaffection.

Gradually the empty houses were occupied. Muslim refugees from Madaripur came in one day and took over several of them. The Banerji mansion was once again filled with people. The Sengupta house near the market was taken by a man called Rafiqul Alam and his family, who had acquired it legally. Mr. Alam, a lawyer, had had a house in a village near Hooghly which he had managed to exchange with the Senguptas.

So Mr. Alam had not had to suffer any loss. Yet, as soon as he came, he started provoking communal antagonism everywhere. Islam was totally endangered in Hindustan, he said; the Muslims hardly dared to set foot in the streets, the Hindus immediately mowed them down; even the police would fire on Muslims as soon as they saw them. Radio Pakistan was also doing its bit through propaganda. A lot of people in the village had managed to acquire cheap American radio sets. And if you listened to Radio Pakistan broadcasts at the time, you thought that India was only a land of bestiality, where aggression was the law.

My father and his friends were so terrified of these broadcasts and their possible repercussions, that they called a meeting under the big banyan tree in our village. The conduct of Hindus in India was severely condemned and even a resolution was passed. But such measures were like attempts to stem the influx of flood by bailing out the onrushing water.

*

You see, I remember everything, not the slightest detail has escaped me, my memory has not lapsed at all. I am lying in a hospital bed in Calcutta. Shukla came and visited me a while back. Haranda, Sukhen, Dibya and some others came in the morning. Apparently, Labonya and her father Biswanath had come to see me yesterday in the afternoon, but I had been asleep. The whole of my head is covered with bandages, my arms are strapped to the bed. But my head itches in a most unbearable fashion. Nurse, why don't you take off this bandage and scratch my head a little? I shall be grateful forever.

When my father died, I did not have to shave my head as is the usual custom. In fact, we were unable to carry out the proper rituals for him. On the eighth day after his death, our house caught fire. We still don't know whether anyone set fire to it deliberately or whether it was just an accident. The foundations were earth, not concrete, the walls made of tin and the roof thatched with hay. Not a scrap of cement or iron anywhere. The whole thing was structured round bamboo poles tied with coir ropes. The slightest spark could ignite it like a matchbox.

My father died of apoplexy. He just went to bed one night and never woke up again. Before this, he had had occasional bouts of asthama, but otherwise he had been in good health. I suppose it was the accumulated toll of poverty, anxiety and fear which caused his death. As I've said earlier, in the days before I was born, or even when I was a baby, my father would leave home and just disappear from time to time. There would be no word from him for three or four months. But of late, he had not been able to do that. For that would have meant the loss of his teaching job, and starvation for his family. But it is always true that a man who is strongly drawn by the world outside, cannot survive long in captivity at home. Perhaps that is why my father left home forever.

Some of the villagers helped us out with money, and we did make arrangements for observing the rituals of the dead. But the fire came before the eleventh day. Even on the day after the fire, we tried to reconstruct our domesticity in the middle of destruction. You are not supposed to leave your home during the period of mourning. So that following night, my mother boiled us some rice and vegetables in an earthenware pot. But that same night several other houses in the village burned down. Dawn saw us leave the village in separate little groups.

The grapefruit tree had escaped the touch of fire. It was loaded with fruit. We left it behind. My brother and I carried two bundles slung from our shoulders. Our mother held our hands firmly. A few steps brought us near Jiban Chakrabarty's famous lime orchard. Now the place had become a wilderness. The fragrant lime trees and the gardenia trees had encroached on each other's preserves. I remember the overpowering, intoxicating smell that used to come to my nostrils in the evenings, whenever I happened to walk past the orchard. Clusters of fire-flies would illuminate the darkness. Could even heaven look more beautiful? Jiban Chakrabarty used to get very angry everytime you plucked a lime from his trees. He would run after you with upraised sandal in hand. Often in the mornings, when our mother gave us last night's soaked rice for breakfast, my brother and I would run to tear some leaves from the lime trees. As soon as you squeezed those leaves, and mixed them with the rice, they gave off a most wonderful flavour. Can I ever forget the smell of those lime leaves?

We went along the raised path beside the narrow canal. On one side were the jute fields, on the other the rice fields. At the edge of the canal, a cane grove housed the nest of bulbuls. I had an impulse to run forward and pluck some ripe cane fruit. But I didn't. It was in those jute fields that Amala*di*'s dismembered body had been discovered. I was afraid to go there.

A little further on, where the road curved, you could see the big banyan tree. At one time this used to be the site where the goddess Kali was worshipped. Wandering gypsies came and pitched their tents here too. During the day, we would come here quite often to play, but at night the place gave me the shivers. There was a deep hole in the massive trunk of the banyan tree. But I had never had the courage to peer inside. We all knew that it housed a *shankhachur* snake, a kind of cobra. Once we had seen a pair of eyes glittering in the darkness of the hole—probably a polecat or a civet cat—but we had pretended it was a real tiger. The village cremation ground was also near the banyan tree. It was only a few days ago that we had cremated my father here. Nobody in the village had died in the last few days. So the remains of our dead, bits and pieces of burnt wood and shards from broken pots—all lay undisturbed. My mother said, 'Don't look that way, don't turn your head. Come along, walk fast.' She had not even had the time to mourn our father. At that point, her only preoccupation was how to save us. So we walked past the banyan tree. After cremating your father, you were supposed to break a pot and walk away from the cremation ground without looking back. We too were leaving our cremation ground behind, never to look back again.

It was not quite daylight. The village was still asleep, the peasants had not come to work in the fields. We left behind the temple of Shiva, the betelnut grove, the big pond—the same pond where I had learnt to swim. The road sloped considerably near the settlement of the untouchables. During the monsoon, rainwater would accumulate here until it blended with the waters of the canal. We had to swim across this place when going to school. Thank God it was not the monsoon now. Ganapati Banerji's house was now full of people, all the weeds and bushes cleared. No doubt his father's ghost had also ceased haunting the place. But even in that house not a soul stirred. We walked past, unobserved.

But there was one person whom we could not escape.

53

Our headmaster Amjad Ali would get up every day at the crack of dawn and stroll down to the canal while brushing his teeth with a twig broken from a *neem* tree. A habit of many years. Suddenly we came face to face with him. The headmaster stopped short in his tracks. His face looked melancholy. After a short silence he spoke to us.

'So you all have decided to leave too?'

We were speechless. My mother was frightened. Everything frightened her now. Her grip on our hands tightened. The headmaster spoke to me.

'Arjun, your exams are only one month away. Will you go away without taking them?'

What could I say in reply? Tears choked my voice, I could hardly look at him. Amjad Ali came forward a few steps and said in a tone of entreaty, 'Please don't go. I myself shall write to the District Board and get funds sanctioned to rebuild your house.'

I don't know whether it was anger or hurt that was uppermost, but our mother suddenly spoke with suppressed violence.

'Don't speak to him, don't say a word. Quick, start walking. Don't keep on standing here.'

She pulled us by the hand. Probably her words reached the headmaster's ears. We moved forward a few steps. My brother only turned his head and said, 'Goodbye sir, we must go.'

Sadly the headmaster said, 'Don't talk about going, say you will be back.'

It was probably out of habit that he said that. It was customary not to speak of going at the time of departure, you were supposed to talk about coming back. But we would never be able to come back again. Those afternoons spent catching fish in the submerged rice fields, the fragrance of lime leaves in the rice, the call of chameleons from the banyan tree, swimming across to school, shivering with fear of the supernatural, climbing the date palm trees to steal the tapped, accumulated juice, accepting sweets from Amala*di*, encountering a chameleon underneath a tree—my native land consisted of all this and so many other images. And I left it behind.

We walked eleven miles to Madaripur. Other groups had come and joined us along the way. Riots had started in Narayanganj, in reprisal against riots in Titagarh near Calcutta. So thousands of helpless people were coming into Madaripur. We had never seen Titagarh, nor had we ever been to Narayanganj; we did not know the people who were killing or being killed in those places. But we had to leave our homes because of them.

The river Ariyal Khan flows past Madaripur, its swift current as potent as its name. Before this, I had come only once to the banks of the Ariyal Khan. I was with my father who had come to buy some *hilsa* fish. I was about five years old. All the fishermen and boatmen took me in their arms and petted me. That was the *hilsa* season. There were countless vessels midstream, all catching fish. The markets were awash with *hilsa*. My father bought a three pound fish for two annas. The fishermen gave us a tiny *hilsa* for free. 'Fry this one whole and give it to the little gentleman, sir' they said to my father.

Now when we came to that same river bank, we had to wait for the steamer, for thirty-six hours we had to sit there. The first steamer did not have room for us. So we slept in the open fields on the river bank. We satisfied our hunger by chewing on flattened, dried rice. After all, we were Brahmins; custom forbade us from cooking in such surroundings, open to possible contamination by other castes. Actually, we did have some rice and foodstuff with us to cook. And, of course, we forgot all such dictates of custom and ritual within a few days.

There were so many people waiting for the steamer, and yet there was hardly any noise, any rush. One and all, they sat there in a mute daze, staring at the river. Waiting for the steamer. I remember my eyes began to hurt from the intensity of staring. To be quite honest, I was still too young, at the age of eleven, to be overwhelmed by the tragedy of leaving my country. There was also an element of excitement, the lure of going to some strange and distant land. So the lack of food and having to sleep in an open field did not make me suffer too much.

The river Ariyal Khan has no associations of holiness

like the Ganges. On the contrary, the recurrence of floods which often disastrously change the course of the river, as well as the frequent incursions by pirates, have given the river a fearful reputation. Yet, it was on the banks of this river that our mother made us complete the final rituals of the dead. Without the benefit of priests and prayers, we just sat on the river bank and made our offerings of soaked rice to the spirit of our dead father. There was no time to shave our heads; the unbleached cloth we had put on to mark the period of mourning was not discarded either. As for eating fish or meat, that came ages later.

There is no point in dwelling on subsequent details. This is not a travelogue. Such experiences of horror and sadness are better left untold.

The steamer brought us to Khulna. There also we encountered masses of people. It was impossible to get on to a train for three days. Many people reached the limits of their patience here, and started fighting and jostling among themselves. One group finally decided they would not wait for the train, but make for the Indian border on foot. We made the mistake of joining them. But what could we have done? There was no one we could turn to for advice. I was eleven, my brother seventeen, and our mother in a daze in these totally unknown surroundings. She had once visited Calcutta in her youth, but that visit had nothing in common with this experience.

We accompanied the group for a while before losing them. That was when we got into real trouble. We had no sense of direction. It is always unnerving to travel on foot through unfamiliar towns and villages. The inhabitants look at you strangely. Even though there had been no riots in Khulna at that time, still it was a time of anarchy and robbery. It is very easy to rob helpless people.

Not that we feared being robbed. We had nothing much to lose except our lives. And our mother was watching out for us with the sharp protective look of a mother bird. No, the danger came from a different quarter.

Two men appeared one day and showed us a great deal

of sympathy. They wanted us to come with them and promised to shelter us. And we did not doubt their kindness either. But my mother was only thirty-four at that time. Her health was still good, her complexion beautifully fair. The people in our village used to say, 'The Raychoudhury bride is just like an image of the goddess Laxmi.' How were we to know that this was a possession sufficient to warrant robbery? The amazing thing was that those two men had realized that we had just lost our father, and their expressions of sympathy were profuse. Yet they had no compunction about coveting our mother. She would not have escaped, nor would we have survived with our lives, had it not been for a stroke of luck. Another group of men turned up with the same motive, and got into a fight with the first two. That is how we managed to get an opportunity to escape.

We left two more villages behind before coming to a huge empty house on the river bank where we took shelter for three days. My mother had sprained her ankle while we were escaping, and by now she was unable to walk. The house must have belonged to some Hindu family, deserted in haste. The doors and windows were still undamaged. For one whole day we just sat there behind barred doors. But we could not continue like that. We had not had a bite to eat for the last four or five days. The rice and provisions we had started out with, had scattered by the wayside—we had absolutely nothing to eat. That was when my brother and I decided to take turns and go begging.

If you are really desperate, you stop fearing even death. We did not know what kind of people the villagers were, certainly we could not have anticipated the new dangers that could befall us at any moment. Yet, the pangs of hunger drove us to plunge into the settlements of the weavers and fishermen and start begging. This was the first time I was doing something like this, yet the art of begging came naturally to me. I would wander from door to door, asking for alms in a piteous, wailing monotone. The sacred thread round my neck, my unkempt hair, and the unbleached cloth I wore, proclaimed that I was a Brahmin boy who had lost his father. Even now, I think, the practice of giving alms to the orphan exists in most communities.

One day, I was given a pound of rice, two aubergines and two potatoes at one of the village houses. What joy that was! I forgot all my sorrows. It seemed I had been granted the most entrancing treasure on earth, the world was full of happiness. What a lovely smell the rice had, the colour of the fresh vegetables so beautiful. I skipped along to our riverside hideout and banged furiously on the door in my excitement. My mother and brother asked in tremulous tones of fear, 'Who is it?'

'It's Arjun. Open the door. Look mother, look at what I have got for you today.'

I cannot remember the name of that sheltering village, but the few days we were there went reasonably well. But then the villagers started to come by and peer inside the house, and worse than that, the police turned up too. So we had to leave. We travelled for a while before encountering another group who were walking to the border. We never lost them. In fact, we are still with them.

None of them had come from our village, but they did belong to our district. Some of them even knew my father. In fact, there was this blind old man who said he had known my father quite well in the days before he had lost his sight. That was when I first met Grandfather Nishi. He used to belong to a group of terrorists at one time, until he was captured by the police and lost his eyesight under torture. He had had to give up his eyes in order to liberate his country; now that the country had gained independence, he was reduced to destitution, forced to leave his home behind and stumble forward in search of some unfamiliar, dark abode. Labonya was about six or seven years old at that time. It was she who used to hold Grandfather Nishi's hand and guide his steps. Grandmother was still alive, but arthritis had robbed her of the power to walk. Uncle Biswanath had to carry her in his arms.

We finally reached Bongaon after crossing the border at Haridaspur. Everyone was overwhelmed with joy. We were safe at last, nobody would come hunting us again. What a marvellous sense of shelter and security. I don't know why, but we thought that as soon as we crossed the border, willing arms would open wide for us, we would be welcomed as brothers. Members of different families would come forward and claim us as their guests. Whenever a newcomer had arrived in our village, it had been the custom of the local families to take turns and invite him to dinner. In the same fashion, we thought, these people here would welcome us and listen eagerly to our tales of exodus.

Several camps had been set up near the station, but there was hardly room to move there. The station platform was swarming with human beings. These uprooted people had taken shelter in neighbouring fields, under the trees. Eating, sleeping, defecating—everything went on in the same place. And, of course, cholera came and carried them off rapidly, one after the other. Labonya's grandmother, having traversed all that distance in her son's arms, finally died in Bongaon. The soil of India did not give her a chance to live.

The volunteers from the Ramkrishna Mission came every day to distribute some rice, lentils and British milk—which is what we called the acutely tasteless powdered milk. But there was always a scramble to get hold of those meagre supplies. Government workers also came every day to count our numbers, and every day they made mistakes.

My brother and I, with our mother, had managed to find a niche in one corner of the platform. In this new country where even the language was hard to understand we could only look on helplessly at everything, a terrible sense of emptiness in our hearts. The local people would come to the overbridge in the station and stand and stare at us, as if we were a new breed of animals. No one came forward to speak to us. No one said, you are our guests, come and have a meal with us at home.

Occasionally, of course, a few people would come to show us their kindness. After dark. They would make whispered propositions to give us jobs. Assurances of safety and shelter to our mother. None of them looked like ordinary people. They were either scrawny and wizened, or obese and gross.

'Here you are my boy, take this,' said one fat man, as he shoved a silver coin into my hand and cast covetous glances at my mother.

But by that time we had become wise in the ways of the world. In spite of being our mother's sons, we had become aware of the value of her youth and beauty. On the way to the border, in the station, we had been forced to hear tales of abduction and rape. Even though we were young boys, nobody had tried to keep those tales of horror from us. For nobody was quite in their right senses. And even here, we had heard of the disappearance of several young girls from some of the families. I did see one of them later. She looked totally distraught. Day and night, the tears dripped from her eyes. Four of those animals had raped her together. Her mother just kept on shrieking curses at her, 'Why couldn't you have died, you disgraceful bitch. It would be a blessing to have you dead.' That poor girl had suffered so much, but what was worse, there was no one to give her any solace.

So, my brother and I guarded our mother like a pair of hunting dogs. Nobody could have laid a finger on her unless they had killed both of us. Whenever anyone said anything insulting, we would bristle. I threw the silver coin given to me by that fat man, straight on to the railway tracks. But, I am not ashamed to admit, later that same night, I descended on to the tracks to search frantically until I recovered the coin. After all, there is nothing more humiliating than having to starve.

From Bongaon, we gradually made our way to Sealdah station in Calcutta. Our sufferings increased. Our days were plagued by flies, and the nights by mosquitoes. Squalor, dirt, noise and the inevitable scramble for food. The local passengers rushed past us without a second look. The unmindful steps of some of them would overturn our cooking pots from time to time. This was the fabled city of Calcutta—but we never had the courage to set foot outside the station. The prolonged lack of food had made my mother emaciated, her youth and beauty had become a thing of the past. So no one came to show us kindness anymore. Once in a while, photographers from newspaper offices would come and take pictures. Well-dressed reporters would come to us, squat on the ground and ask us tricky questions—we did not feel the need to answer. When they went away, we would start bemoaning our fate in whispers. But there was one man among us whom I never heard lamenting, and this was old, blind Grandfather Nishi. Sometimes, in the middle of the night, I even heard him hum 'Bande Mataram', one of our rousing nationalist songs.

Finally, however, we came to the limits of our endurance. We had heard many rumours by then—of plans to send us to settle in the Andaman Islands, or Dandakaranya. But nothing was actually being done. Occasionally a man would come and make a speech about no Bengalis being forced to move out of Bengal. Yet another would come and proclaim that the Indian government had betrayed us by refusing to take responsibility for us. But all that was over our heads. All we wanted then was space to lie on our backs, a roof of some sort over our heads, two meals a day and some privacy. Before this exodus, my mother had never gone out in front of strangers, and now a thousand eyes were turned on her.

This was the point at which Biraj Thakur appeared before us. A man of mystery. The members of our present colony still talk about him. Yet, later on, he disappeared completely, we never heard of him again. He did not belong to any political party either, for somebody would surely have said so.

He was very tall and fair. Blind in one eye. With a loud, raucous voice, which gave you no opportunity to think that this man was capable of kindness or benevolence. All of a sudden, one morning, he called all the adults in our group together around himself. His manner was not that of an unknown political leader. Rather, it was like that of a village headman, who could tell us off in no uncertain terms. We children also tried to hover on the outskirts of the group and overhear things.

He certainly was taller than any one of us. Blind in one eye, but possessed of unusual brilliance in the other. He wore a *dhoti* and a half-sleeved shirt, and he did not squat. He sat down flat on the dust of the platform, along with us. He shouted at us in that harsh voice of his.

'What do you think you are doing? Do you want to just sit and rot here? Are you men or just animals? Have you left your own homes behind only to come and beg here? Don't you have a right to the soil of this country? Do you know what will happen if you just keep on sitting here? The children will scavenge in the streets, the young girls will become whores and the rest of you beggars. Well, why don't you open your mouths?'

And Biraj Thakur went on, 'Nobody shows you pity when you beg for it. How long can you sit and wait for the government to take pity on you and send you somewhere? And why should you have to squabble among yourselves every time the government doles out a handful of rice or two rupees in cash? Are you a race of beggars? Isn't this your own country? It was not your fault that the country was partitioned. The more you delay, the worse off you will be. You just can't afford to sit back and wait, you must fight for your rights. You will have to work hard to achieve self-reliance, but you can do it. There is a lot of land on the outskirts of Calcutta, and quite a few unoccupied country houses. I know them all. Come with me. You must force your way in. If anyone tries to stop you, fight to the death, but do not give up your land.'

It took Biraj Thakur many days to make his ideas acceptable to us. To the people of East Bengal, the right to land was a sacred right. They still believe that. These people who had been forced to leave their own land behind, still shrank from acquiring other people's land by force. Besides, nobody really knew Biraj Thakur. Who knew what kind of trouble they could get into if they were led by him? But finally, all these doubts and hesitations had to give way. We had come to such a pass that we could not contemplate anything being worse. Early one morning we set out with Biraj Thakur. He just came to us and announced 'Those of you who want to follow me, come along now. And those of you who want to become beggars can stay back. Come!'

Not a single soul was left behind.

I don't suppose one could have called that a procession. We had not learned the art of walking together in an orderly fashion. Just a group of men and women rushing along the streets—three thousand in all. My brother held our mother's hand. I was guiding Grandfather Nishi along. Dibya had got hold of a broken stick from somewhere and was brandishing it with glee. You would have thought from his enthusiasm that he was setting forth on a conquest. Mile after mile flashed by, we were running, panting for breath, and yet we did not stop.

Then we came to a suburb in Dum Dum and, sure enough, there were quite a few of those country homes. Biraj Thakur divided us into groups and allotted each one a house and a garden. We did not meet with resistance. The property that we entered did have two guards, but they disappeared in the rush of this tide of humanity.

We could not even have dreamt of such a wonderful place of refuge. This beautiful garden, surrounded by many kinds of trees—it reminded us of our village. True, there was a chance of bickering over the occupancy of the dance hall. For everyone wanted to possess the one concrete building. Finally, it was Grandfather Nishi who gave us the solution. Brahmins had always been well-respected in East Bengal. It was often customary to call in Brahmins from other places and give them land to settle in a village. There were two Brahmin families in our group, ours and Haranda's. they had been priests by profession, and my father had been a school teacher. So these two families were given the dance hall, in keeping with their special status as Brahmins. The understanding was that once the colony established a school of its own, my brother and I would have to teach there. And Haranda was entrusted with the responsibility of carrying out religious rites for the living and the dead.

That was how a group of destitute people found a new place to settle. Having left their own land behind, they named this place 'Deshpran Colony' or the colony of patriots. We never heard of Biraj Thakur again. Why he had suddenly appeared to help us, and why he chose to

63

disappear—these are questions to which we don't have the answer. Later on, of course, a few political parties claimed that they were responsible for our refuge and tried to acquire the rights of supervision over us. But we know for sure that Biraj Thakur had never belonged to any one of them. There is an altar built underneath the huge mango tree beside our pond, with his name engraved on it. Later in life, when I read the biography of Che Guevera, I was reminded of Biraj Thakur. That tall figure, blind in one eye, harsh of expression, yet so noble.

Appreciation of our wonderful new home overwhelmed us. We were always on the lookout for attempts to drive us out again. Groups of people would guard the colony day and night. Having been fellow travellers on the road of suffering gave us a tremendous feeling of solidarity among ourselves. The men used to stay up at night and stand guard with sticks in their hands. Even we boys did our share. Dibya had already become a big, strapping young fellow. It was natural for him to be called in whenever anything difficult needed to be done. And he himself had no hesitation in stepping forward to help in times of trouble. We used to practise the use of sticks in defence every morning, as a part of our physical fitness regimen. But Grandfather Nishi always warned us against any excess.

'Never pick a fight with outsiders,' he said, 'without a very good reason. We have come here, a new place; we must make ourselves accepted. The local people must learn to like us.'

That was only about fifteen years ago. So many changes have taken place since then. I set foot in this city not knowing which way to turn, and now it has become familiar territory, my own pasture. I do not have a moment's hesitation in thinking of it as my own city. Everyone in the colony has succeeded in finding his or her own means of livelihood. In the beginning some of us worked as porters in the market, waiters in the teashops and rickshaw pullers. Some even went out begging. But look at us now. Some run their own business, a few have found jobs in bakeries and plywood factories. Haranda did not continue to be our priest—he drives a taxi. There is also a school teacher and a couple of clerks.

I myself worked as a waiter in a teashop for the first few months. I was paid a monthly salary of twelve rupees, which came to about twenty-five rupees with tips. Plus, I was given a free meal a day. On the days when I managed to get hold of some leftover meat, I would bring it home and share it with my brother.

I still remember clearly how my wits sharpened in the course of my apprenticeship at the shop. If I noticed a group of customers sitting at a table for a long time and chatting, I would go up to them and ask, 'Would you like anything more, sir? Shall I bring you something?' This pleased the owner of the teashop. It also attracted the attention of the owner of the Punjabi shop across the street. He tried to lure me away with the bribe of a bigger salary. I resisted for a while, then went. The bearded old Punjabi shopkeeper really grew to be very fond of me. He never scolded me. Long after I stopped working for him, the old man would invite me into his shop whenever he saw me passing by, and give me a meal without charging me for it. One benefit of working there was that I could bring home curried meat quite often—whatever was left over in the kitchens. My brother was always delighted with that. I did not get too many opportunities to please him.

My mother, of course, was entirely against my working. She used to weep bitterly over it. She knew that I had brains. I could do a lot if I was given the chance to study. Whereas, if I stuck to working in a teashop, I would probably do so for the rest of my days. Besides, it was possible for me to get free admission in any school, for boys who stood at the top of their class always got tuition waivers. My mother was a very good seamstress. Uncle Biswanath got her a contract with a tailor's shop to sew shirts and trousers. A short time after that, I was admitted to school, having lost a year in between. I knew then that I had to work desperately hard—that was my only weapon to ensure victory, there was no other way for us to survive. So I electrified the whole colony by getting the second place in the final school-leaving exams.

See, I remember everything. My memory is intact, nothing is forgotten. But I wonder who could have hit me like this. I have never harmed anyone.

III

Dibya was going along to the pond, holding the dead snake on the edge of a raised stick. A host of children trailed along behind him. Dibya had been looking out for the snake for quite a few days. Once he was obsessed with something, he would never stop until satisfied. It was a huge snake, non-poisonous, but any part of your body that was touched by the thrashing tail would rot.

Grandfather Nishi put his hand on Naru's shoulder and asked, 'What is all that noise about? Naru, why do the boys shout so?'

'Dibya*da* has killed a snake,' said Naru. 'A huge big one.'

He extended his hands to approximate the length, even though his grandfather could not see the gesture.

'Good God, what kind of a snake was it? Did anybody get bitten?'

'No, no. You just stay here. I'll run over and take a quick look.'

'Can't you see from here? Well then, take me along with you.'

'How will that help? You just stay here.'

It was the time of day when the colony was quiet and peaceful. The older men were mostly at work while the young men, who were mostly unemployed, would stand around talking in the street in front of the colony. Somehow, it had become the practice for the boys to go to school for a while, then quit when they got to the last one or two grades, and start looking for jobs in the neighbouring factories. Some of them tried to open shops, some became real toughs, and a few just disappeared. The few boys who graduated from high school and went to the university stopped speaking to the rest. There were also a few girls who went to work in the city; some of them even worked in the evening shifts.

Dibya was one of those who hated to waste time sitting around and gossiping. He wanted to have something to do, all the time. That was why he was so enthusiastic over hunting down the snake. It was not wise to leave a dead snake lying around. They were supposed to revive with the rain, or so the superstition went. So Dibya was making arrangements to burn the snake on the banks of the pond. He collected a pile of twigs and bits of wood and set fire to it. The girls had come to the pond to bathe, and do their washing. They gazed at him with wondering fascination. The rubbery corpse of the snake was difficult to burn. Everyone had thought the snake was absolutely dead. Yet, the touch of fire still made its body writhe.

Dibya had quite a reputation for hunting and killing snakes. Once a snake had been sighted in the compound of the Mitras' house, on the other side of the street. Everyone saw the snake glide past and hide under the stairs. That was it. They were terrified of climbing up and down those stairs. That was when Dibya had been called in. Of course, it was child's play to him. He wrapped a piece of burlap round his hand, went round to the back of the staircase, and came out dragging the snake by its tail. He might even have been given some sort of a reward for his courage, except that he held the snake up close to the face of Mr Mitra's daughter-in-law and scared her. They all became so angry at his impudence, that nothing was offered to him. Not that Dibya ever expected any rewards.

Labonya was walking along the other side of the pond. There was another girl in the neighbouring colony who was about to take the BA degree examinations. Labonya had gone over to exchange books and notes with her. As she walked, a huge frond of coconut leaf fell down right in front of her. It escaped hitting her on the head by inches. Labonya was a bit scared at first, but she recovered soon enough. She grabbed hold of the stem and started dragging it home. It would come in useful. Dibya saw her and called out, 'Labi, bring that thing along here. I am having trouble getting a good fire going.'

'No', said Labonya, 'I can't let you have this one. It will make a wonderful broom.'

'What do you want with yet another broom? Do you want to hit some luckless fellow with it?'

Labonya smiled and said, 'Well, don't worry, whoever it may be, it's not you.'

'As if I am scared of you. Now then, bring it along here.'

'No, I won't. I got it first.'

But if Dibya wanted something, it was in his nature to make sure he got it. He ran towards Labonya. The snake-burning being a lot of fun, a group of little boys also rushed forward behind him. Labonya let the coconut leaf go before Dibya could put his hand on it. He smiled at that.

'What's come over you Labi? Why do you answer back so often these days?'

Labonya smiled back at him.

'Why not?' she said. 'Do I have to be afraid of you?'

'That you can find out my girl, any time you like.'

And Dibya raised his fist playfully in the air, but Labonya moved aside in a flash. He called after her again.

'Don't go off like that Labi. Listen, there's something I want to discuss with you.'

But Labonya didn't reply. She walked rapidly to the dance hall, climbed up on to the porch and started talking to Arjun's mother.

Shanti*pishi*, when is Arjun*da* expected back?

Dibya stood by the pond, looked around and saw the manager of the plywood factory, Kewal Singh, standing a little way off, talking to some people from the colony. He averted his gaze and came back with his new fuel to replenish the fire.

*

The boundary wall of the colony had been reduced to rubble in many places. So the plywood factory at the back had almost merged with the colony. The five families who lived near it had no privacy anymore. The people in the factory could look straight into their rooms and watch them cooking, eating, sleeping. Whenever the women came near a door, or a window, hungry eyes licked them all over.

You need a lot of open space to dry sheets of plywood. Gradually the sheets had spilled over from the factory area into the colony. Flat, square, white pieces of wood were spread out on the ground within the colony, and the factory workers kept coming and going. In fact, such was the frequency of their movements, that they stepped carelessly across the little garden plots owned by the colony members. Sometimes, a few of the men would even sit next to somebody's room to have a smoke and talk in sinister whispers.

A few small children were playing hopscotch over the pieces of wood. The square boards arranged in neat proximity easily lent themselves to the imagination as the squares on a hopscotch court. Soon the boards were covered with small, dusty footprints, rather like a traditional pattern of the goddess Laxmi's footprints. Suddenly some labourers from the factory rushed out trying to catch the children. Most of them escaped, but one got his ears boxed and his face slapped so hard that the marks of fingers showed on his cheek. It is true, of course, that the boy had put his tongue out at the labourers as he had tried to escape. He burst out crying and ran into his house.

Shortly afterwards, Dhiren Shikdar came out of the same house and let loose a flood of abuse. Three children had died before Dhiren Shikdar had had this son born to him, late in life. Nobody at home would lay a finger on the boy. Yet, these uncouth labourers from the factory had had the nerve to hit him. Dhiren kept on shouting at the top of his voice,

'You bastards, you good for nothing sons of Marwaris, how dare you touch my son? Do you think I live off your earnings? You sons of bitches, come on out here and I

70

will smash your ugly faces.'

Haradhan Ray came out of the neighbouring house asking, 'What is the matter, Dhiren?'

'Will you just look at the nerve of these people? They've beaten my poor little Nimai so hard, the child is now hiccuping with fear.'

'Why did they have to do that?'

'Don't you know why? Don't our kids have the right to play on our land? But no, those hulks had to come here and...'

'Yes, you are dead right. These people are getting to be too big for their boots.'

Dhiren Shikdar started cursing again with Haradhan supporting him, when, suddenly, Kewal Singh came out of the factory and started walking towards them. Immediately they were silenced. Basically they were cowards. However much they shouted and raved, it took only the sight of a big strong man to take the wind out of their sails.

Kewal Singh came up to them with a smile, asking, 'What is it? Dhiren*babu*, what is the matter? Why are you shouting like that?'

Dhiren's voice immediately went down several scales.

'Well, look here Mr. Singh, why should the men from your factory come and beat up my little boy? What right do they have to do this?'

Kewal Singh's eyes dilated to express a most ungodly amazement.

'My men!' he said, 'beat up your boy! Never. Just show me which one it was, and I'll thrash him in front of you.'

It took only these empty words of reassurance to make Dhiren's resentment disapper. He showed no more enthusiasm for the actual carrying out of the retribution. Wasn't it enough for such a big, strong man to give some importance to what he, Dhiren, had been saying? Kewal Singh started speaking again.

'My men cannot have hurt your boy. Kids will often fight among themselves, you know.'

Dhiren made a half-hearted protest.

'No, no, it wasn't like that at all. It was your people who beat him. I saw it with my own eyes.'

'No one in my factory would ever dare do such a thing. But never mind. Oh dear, this is really too bad though. Look how filthy these boards have become. That was why I asked you all to move your houses backward. I would pay all the costs you know.'

'How can we move our houses? Does anyone in his senses pull down his own home?'

'Yes, yes, you all keep saying that. But this is such a good time for business. It would be to your advantage as well as mine.'

What Kewal Singh really wanted was to expand his business. He was having a good run of luck. But the only way he could expand was by going inside the colony. He had proposed that the five or six families in the part of the colony adjacent to the factory move their houses to the unoccupied area near the pond. He was prepared to pay all expenses. After all, houses for these people meant only earth foundations and bamboo walls. It should be no trouble to move them.

While the families concerned found this an extremely dangerous proposal, they still did not have the courage to disregard it totally. Though they had been living in the colony for fifteen years, they had not yet received legal rights of occupancy to it. The real owners of the whole estate had not yet come to a settlement with the government. So not only were the colony members worried about inhabiting a place to which they had no legal rights, they were also scared of having an open confrontation with Kewal Singh. Both Kewal Singh and most of his factory workers were non-Bengalis. So far, though, there had been no serious disagreements between them. Nor did the refugee settlers have any disagreements or even social interaction with the Bengalis outside their colony.

Haradhan Ray had been leaning against his door all through this exchange with Kewal Singh. Not a word passed his lips. He had a houseful of children. His two sons, Kartik and Shibu, were unemployed young men. His daughter Purnima, however, did work part-time in the afternoons. All of them had crowded near the window to listen. Kartik came out now and glared balefully at Kewal Singh.

'Why should we move our houses? This is sheer anarchy. Do you think this is your land, that you are ordering us around?'

Kewal Singh smiled sweetly.

'No, of course not. This is your land, and your forefathers' too. Why should I try to order you around?'

The allusion to their forefathers hit them hard. Dhiren and Haradhan were totally silenced. But Kartik could not contain himself. His voice rose in anger.

'Well, do you think you have inherited this land from *your* forefathers? You are really overstepping the limits these days.'

'Land can only belong to those who have paid for it. Do you think land can be acquired free?'

Haradhan pushed his son aside, saying, 'Kartik, for God's sake go inside.'

'Why should I go in? Do you think I am scared of this Punjabi fellow?'

'Just go inside, will you.'

'You know,' said Kewal Singh, 'I can take out a lease from the real owner of the property. But I thought perhaps it was better to have a straightforward deal between ourselves.'

'Stop talking nonsense,' retorted Kartik. 'Don't give us all this stuff about the real owner. Fat lot of good it will do you, getting a lease from him. Has he done anything about his land in all these years?'

'Please Kartik, why don't you go inside?'

'Stop pushing me around, Father. Arjun was dead right. If we once let go of our land for a bit of money, we shall be in real danger.'

*

At one time, everyone used to compare Shantilata to the image of the goddess Laxmi. If you leave an image outdoors for a long time, the sun and the rain will discolour it. That was how she looked now. She still wore those old-fashioned chemises instead of blouses, and saris made of white unbleached cotton.

73

About a year ago, Arjun had bought his mother a sewing machine with his scholarship money. She had had to rent a machine before that for her work. She always sewed with great patience and concentration. Nobody had ever been able to find fault with her work. She was making a shirt out of fine cotton, when Labonya asked from the porch,

'Shanti*pishi*, when is Arjun*da* coming home?'

Shantilata stopped the machine.

'Is that you Labi?' she said. 'Come in. Arjun should be back tomorrow.'

It was impossible to guess from Shantilata's face the number of sorrows that had befallen her. A serene face, with no trace of anxiety. Though she had managed to overcome the unhappiness of her husband's death fifteen years ago, she still found it impossible to forget the cruel death of her eldest son. But her tears were shed in private. No one had ever seen any signs of weakness in her. Shantilata never complained of being unwell. She was never sick. She had staked all her hopes on Arjun's success.

When the news of Arjun's being injured had been brought to her in the neighbouring colony, as she attended the reading session of the *Mahabharata*, she had thought for a moment that he was dead. That was why she had fainted immediately. But as soon as she recovered she had rushed home, and it was she who had taken charge of organizing medical care and getting him to the hospital. She had had to leave home a helpless, young widow. But she was no longer like that and had acquired the ability to take control of situations with a firm hand.

The things in Arjun's little room, his small bed, his table and stacks of books, were all arranged neatly. The dog was tied to the leg of the table from where it was making a futile effort to catch a cockroach. Shantilata was a Hindu widow, but she was not repelled by the dog, did not consider it unclean. The animal had been a favourite of her son, Somnath, his constant companion.

There was no bed in Shantilata's room. She still made her bed on the floor. In one corner stood two trunks, cheap things picked up second-hand. In another corner, within an alcove, were the earthen images of the goddesses Saraswati and Laxmi, as well as that of the god Narayana. There was also a clothes-hanger and several pieces of cloth lying here and there.

Labonya came in and sat down on the floor by Shantilata. She spoke in a very intimate tone.

'Shanti*pishi*, did you have anything to eat last night?'

'Of course,' smiled Shantilata. 'Why?'

'Come on now, I want the truth. Did you really eat dinner?'

'Yes, my dear, I did. There was some sago I had kept soaked, and I had that with coconut and sugar puffs. Why didn't you come along? I could have given you some.'

'I couldn't. Grandfather was sick.'

'How is he?'

'Oh, much better this morning. I saw that he wasn't running a temperature any longer. I told him not to go out today, but he wouldn't listen. Shanti*pishi*, who turned off your light last night?'

'Why, you think I can't do it myself?'

'I know you can't. Arjun*da* always turns off the light in your room.'

Electric light had come to the colony only a year ago. Shantilata had still not been able to get used to it. She had the habit of leaving a dimly lit lantern near her head when she fell asleep. Total darkness unnerved her. And she was also scared of switching off the light and then walking across the room to her bed. Now, she looked very embarrassed.

'I didn't switch the lights off last night. I slept with them on.'

'But how could you sleep with the light on all night?'

'My dear child, it was better than being totally in the dark. By the way, Labi, I hear that your marriage has been arranged.'

'Who told you? Nothing has been fixed yet.'

'Why, it was your mother. She had come to the reading session yesterday.'

'No, *Pishi*. I don't want to get married yet. Why don't you talk to my mother.'

75

'But why shouldn't you get married now? You are old enough.'

'That's nonsense. I am not all that old. I am only twenty-one.'

'Do you know how old I was when I got married? I was only thirteen. And by the time I was your age, or maybe a couple more years older, I had had both my children.'

'But that was your generation. That was different. I want to continue with my studies.'

'Your exams are not that far off. You can get married after that.'

'No, I want to study some more.'

'How much more can a woman do? Excessive studying is supposed to addle your brains.'

'Well, if you really think that, how come you didn't allow Arjun*da* to take a job after he got his Master's? Why does he continue with his studies?'

'He is a man. It can't be the same for you.'

'Why not?' burst out Labonya passionately. 'I want to pursue higher studies just like Arjun*da*. I want to do research too'

Shantilata did not say any more. She just looked at Labonya tenderly. Labonya was scratching the floor with a downcast face. Arjun had made Labonya realize that only education could raise her above circumstances in the colony. Most of the other members of the colony wandered around, looking for odd jobs; some sold vegetables, some were gratified to get a job in the factory—and these were the concerns which gave rise to factions and arguments. But look at Arjun. He knew so many wonderful people in the city. Some of them even came to see him here, though otherwise they would never have set foot in a colony like this. Labonya wanted to become Arjun's equal.

It was not very realistic for inhabitants of colonies like these to have any ambition. Survival itself was an achievement. After all, how much more was there left to ask, for people who had eluded death and traversed grim distances? Girls like Labonya hardly ever studied beyond high school. Then they got married to boys from other colonies. Some girls did try to get odd jobs, while some others went a different way, coerced by the needs of the body. But Arjun had made Labonya realize that there were other ways of living.

When Arjun had stood second in the final school-leaving examinations, everyone in the colony had thought he would get a good job as a senior clerk in an office. A boy who had a mentally unbalanced brother, and whose mother had to take in work as a seamstress, could expect no greater good fortune. But Arjun had amazed everybody by going to college. Not only that, he did not look for a job even after getting his MSc degree. He knew so many people in Calcutta. He was no longer a person from the colony alone, he had become a citizen of the country he now lived in. Labonya wanted a life like that.

But Labonya was not very bright. She had not been able to do too well in the school-leaving examinations. She had failed in the second part of the Bachelor's examination too. Yet she had an obstinate resolve—to study, to do research—so that people would treat her with respect. Nobody had done so, this far. That was why Labonya used every free moment to sit and memorize her text-books.

'I have heard,' said Shantilata, 'that your future husband is quite well off. Not much older than you either. He has an electrical shop in Patipukur.'

'No,' said Labonya fiercely, 'I won't get married. Nothing will make me do it. What, marry a shopkeeper and...'

At this point Haran poked his head inside.

'Kakima,' said he, 'when will Arjun be coming back? Let me know, so I can go and fetch him in my taxi.'

Haran was a taxi driver. It was considered a great honour for somebody if Haran gave him a free ride in his taxi. The simple fact that he could drive a motor vehicle around, wherever he wanted to, even bring it into the colony from time to time, made many people show considerable deference to Haran. The son of a priest, Haran himself used to officiate at religious ceremonies as late as four years ago. But compared to the respect shown to him then, his social standing within the colony was much higher now.

Not that Haran relinquished any of his pride in being a Brahmin. He had to go to all sorts of places in his taxi, the luxury of insisting on properly cooked food was not for him—but he never missed a chance to convey to you the fact that Brahmins were the most superior beings on earth. It was his Brahmin birth that had got him the right to stay in the only concrete building in the colony. He firmly believed that Arjun's academic brilliance was due to his Brahmin heritage, and that he, Haran, too would not have done too badly if he had pursued an academic career. However, driving a taxi was not much worse than higher studies. It required a special kind of expertise. Nowadays, a marriage or any other kind of ceremony in the colony did not have Haran as the officiating priest. But he did stand around in a pair of khaki trousers and vest, supervising everything. A partiality for locally brewed drinks gave Haran's eyes a bloodshot look most of the time.

'He is supposed to come home tomorrow afternoon,' said Shantilata.

'Let me know for sure by tomorrow morning. I shall go and get him. Labi, would you like to come with me?'

Labonya had adjusted her sari in front as soon as she saw Haran and she sat primly now, with her legs crossed. Even while he was talking about Arjun, Haran's eyes could not stay away from Labonya's breasts and waist.

'No, I don't want to,' said Labonya.

'Why not? It will be a nice drive for you, a bit of fresh air.'

'No, you'd better take Shanti*pishi*. She has not been to the hospital once in all these days.'

'Of course she can come too. Would you like to, *Kakima*?'

Haran now came into the room and planted himself firmly on the floor in front of the two women. He had three children of his own. At this moment two of them were fighting over something, and the other one had been wailing for sometime. And Haran sat here, with expectant, narrowed eyes—just in case Labonya's sari slipped aside, just in case one of the buttons on her blouse was unfastened.

Sometimes, Haran would spend the night away from home. But no one could ever charge him with playing around with the girls in his colony. He had established adoptive relationships of sister, sister-in-law, and aunt with every woman there. But there was no harm in looking, was there? Looks did not wear away anything. Whenever he was off duty, he spent most of his time on the bathing steps near the pond, talking about domestic matters with his sisters and aunties.

Shantilata suddenly remembered something.

'Labi, do you have a coconut grater at home?'

'Yes.'

'Can you go and get it for me? Arjun loves to eat coconut sweets. I managed to get hold of two coconuts yesterday.'

'Why don't you wait a few more days before making them? Do you think the doctors will allow him to eat coconut sweets?'

'You just go and get the grater. That boy loves those sweets. And anyhow, doctors never forbid you anything made by your mother.'

In one respect, Labonya was quite relieved to get up and leave. She was not enjoying being looked at greedily by Haran. But a few steps from there brought her face to face with Sukhen. Casting a quick, furtive look all around, he spoke to her in a low voice.

'Labi, you know Dibya sent for you this morning. Why didn't you go and see him?'

Labonya scowled at him.

'Liar,' she said. 'I met Dibya*da* a little while ago. He never said a word about it.'

Sukhen looked around again.

'It's true', he said. 'Dibya was in our house then. He said to me, "Go and get Labonya. I need her to write a letter for me. She writes well."'

'You think I have nothing better to do than sit and write your letters for you?'

'Why do you always lose your temper so quickly? Have you seen the film, *The Saint and The Merchant*? Do you want to come to the matinee today?'

'No. How many times have I told you, I don't want to go to a film with you.'

'Well, if you change your mind, come to the theatre. Dibya will be there too.'

'If you are that keen for company, why don't you ask Purnima? She's always ready to be asked out.'

'Come on, who wants Purnima? She'd go with anybody. I only want you. I keep trying to tell you so often—but you never take any notice of me.'

'Listen, you come and annoy me once again, and I'll tell Dibya*da*.'

'But it was Dibya who sent me to you. We know you don't get a chance to go the movies.'

'In that case, go and tell Dibya*da* to come and tell me himself. Why have you come?'

'I see. You are getting much too arrogant these days. The only person you care for, is Arjun, isn't it? Well let me tell you, Arjun couldn't care less.'

Anger brought the red blood rushing to Labonya's face.

'Shall I call my father?' She screamed at Sukhen. 'Shall I? You envious, cowardly, creep.'

Sukhen disappeared with alacrity. He wanted to marry Labonya. He did have a job at the bakery worth a hundred and fifteen rupees a month. But his whole appearance was so much at odds with Labonya's blooming health and vigour, that her father himself had rejected the proposal. But still Sukhen could not give up hope. Every time he got her to himself, he tried out his blandishments. But not being courageous, he always dragged Dibya's name into it. He felt that if Dibya managed to make good with Labonya, he would also get a minor share of the spoils.

Gloom descended on Labonya. Nobody loved her, or treated her with respect. Just because she had good health, her body aroused the desire of every male, old or young. God, how small-minded they were! To even hint of something so ugly in connection with Arjun*da*.

Haradhan Ray was standing under the mango tree. Everyone knew he was a petty thief. He was nearly sixty, with very dignified looks—but every time he visited a house, he was sure to take something away. Even a teacup or a glass was not beyond him. But he had a whole houseful of sons, daughters and grand-children. So nobody wanted to catch him and disgrace him in public. Haradhan saw Labonya and spoke in honeyed tones.

'How are you, my dear Labonya? Where have you been?'

'Over at the dance hall, to see Shanti*pishi*.'

'I see. How is Arjun? Have you heard anything?'

'He's fine.'

'Good, very good. What was Sukhen saying to you?'

Labonya scowled again. Even this old uncle was not looking at her face, he too was busy surveying her body with his eyes. Labonya could see through everyone now. She knew what was going on. She had no desire to stand here and talk to this man. So she replied carelessly.

'Oh he was trying to tell me something about your daughter Purnima. I didn't bother to listen.'

She stepped forward to go, but Haradhan called out again.

'Listen my dear, I have something to tell you.'

'What is it? I have an errand to run, Uncle.'

As if the reference to Purnima had escaped him completely, Haradhan started on his speech calmly.

'It does one good even to look at you. A gem of a girl. About to get your BA degree so soon. And you are a girl too. There aren't many boys here who have done as much.'

'Uncle I must go now.'

'Are you managing well with you work? The power cuts come so often now.'

'Yes, I am managing.'

'That's good. Where is your father? At home?'

'No, my father is supposed to be in his shop now.'

'I see.'

Labonya started forward once more, but once again Haradhan called her back.

'Where are you off to now child? Home?'

'Yes, I have to get something for Shanti*pishi*. I am in a hurry. Do you want to tell me anything?'

'No, oh no. There's nothing special to say. It's nice to have a chat with you. You are just as blessed with looks as with abilities, my dear. Girls like you...'

Then with the look of someone suddenly reminded of something, Haradhan lowered his voice to ask, 'Do you have four annas to spare? I could give it back to you tomorrow morning. I don't have any change you see, and I need to buy some cigarettes.'

'No, I don't have any money.'

*

Haradhan moved forward with tranquil, deliberate steps, as if nothing mattered to him in this world. He had asked for a petty loan and been refused curtly—but it did not matter. Life was an illusion, anyway. He looked at the houses in the colony, at the trees, as if the sight gave him pleasure. There were two coconut trees growing side by side bearing coconuts. He stopped for a while to count the coconuts.

There was a small crowd in front of Biswanath's drycleaning shop. Biswanath himself did not much care to have these daily gatherings at his shop, but there was nothing he could do about it. Some barged straight into the shop, others sat down outside on the wooden platform. The platform had been built over an open sewer, to provide a foundation for the shop, and Biswanath did not pay rent for the shop either. So he was in no position to claim it as his own private territory.

Haradhan walked into the shop stood next to Biswanath and spoke to him in tones of the greatest friendship.

'Let's have a cigarette. I haven't had a cigarette off you for days.'

Biswanath was a dour sort of person. He had been turning over the pages of the account book. Now he did not even look at Haradhan to answer him.

'The cigarette shop is just down the road. Why don't you go and buy some?'

'No, I want one of yours. They have a special taste. Don't you understand, the taste of something that doesn't belong to you. Ha, ha, ha...'

'I don't smoke cigarettes, only *bidis*.'

'Oh, that's all the same, my dear fellow. When we were in the village, we hardly ever saw a cigarette. *Bidis* are our authentic cigarettes.'

Lighting the *bidi* Biswanath gave him, Haradhan took a puff with great relish. He decided to be nice to Biswanath, flatter him a little.

'You really are having to work hard these days, aren't you? I see that you have lots of customers these days too. But of course, that means the shop has taken off the ground. What do you say?'

Biswanath said shortly that he was just about breaking even in the business.

'Biswanath, I have a private matter to discuss with you.'

'What is it?'

Even as he worked, Biswanath remained watchful, so that pencils, pens, or other such things did not disappear from the counter into Haradhan's pocket. The cashbox was locked.

'Promise me you won't be angry? And that you won't tell anyone?'

'But tell me what it's all about.'

'You must lend me five rupees today. You just have to. I won't leave until you do.'

'Forgive me Haradhan*da*, I have lent you money often before. Now I have trouble myself making both ends meet.'

'Softly, softly. There's no need to let other people hear all this.'

The crowd swelled again in front of the shop. Dibya had come up, and several people surrounded him. Now that the snake had been disposed of, Dibya was looking for something else to do. Haradhan raised his voice to speak to Dibya.

'Dibya, why did you have to go and burn that huge snake? I've heard that snake skin can fetch high prices.'

'Perhaps, perhaps,' said Dibya sarcastically. 'But I am not a butcher, so you can hardly expect me to know about the skin trade.'

'Of course not. I only mentioned it. And this I'll say

the skin trade.'

'Of course not. I only mentioned it. And this I'll say Dibya, nobody else could have killed that enormous snake. You really are a pillar of strength to us. But I don't understand how anybody could have come and beaten up Arjun the way they did, when there are people like you around.'

This embarrassed Dibya. For this was one mystery he had not been able to solve. Dibya had been invested with the role of protector of the colony because of his sheer physical prowess. So any occurrence of violence seemed to add to his responsibilities. But this last incident was something he had not been able to do anything about. It was true that he had had his share of childhood squabbles with Arjun, but at the bottom of his heart, he had a great deal of respect for Arjun. The newspapers had printed Arjun's photograph three times already; when Arjun stood second in the final school-leaving exams, there had even been a write-up on the colony in the papers. Sometimes when there was an argument with boys from the neighbouring colony, Dibya would end up by saying, 'Go on, what do you think you are? Nobody has even heard of you lot. But our Arjun went up to get a certificate from the President of India himself. And the President bowed to him too. Do you think any of you will ever get your pictures in the paper?'

Now Dibya tried to find an excuse.

'That was during the blackout. We were all involved with the taxi driver then.'

'Do you think it was anybody from our colony? Or was it someone from outside?'

'Someone from the colony beat up Arjun! What are you saying Haradhan*da*?'

'It's always hard to know what people are really like, my boy. These days people have so many motives. I don't care what you say, but that Kewal Singh fellow is not to be trusted. Why don't you put him in his place?'

Most people in the colony disliked Kewal Singh. But he was a wily person and had managed to get the young people on his side. He was on reasonably good terms with Dibya.

'He hasn't done us any harm,' said Dibya. 'And he gives us a fifty-rupee subscription for our Saraswati Puja festival.'

A boy called Shashadhar spoke up at this point. In his opinion, Arjun was spending too much time with a rich man's daughter. So it must have been the girl's father who had hired thugs to beat him up. Shashadhar had come across this kind of melodramatic plot in a recent Hindi film. But Dibya dismissed him easily.

'What nonsense. Who's been talking to you about Arjun?'

'I tell you, I've seen it with my own eyes. Arjun was driving with a girl in a white car. And that girl visits him in hospital too. I've heard her uncle is a minister.'

Biswanath never joined in such discussions. He was cutting up pieces of paper with numbers written on them and tagging laundered clothes for identification. He had absolutely no enthusiasm for this kind of gossip about other people. He was amazed that even now, people could not pursue their own ends, but wasted time over the affairs of others. But he was not to be left in peace. Haradhan started on him again in a low voice.

'You see Biswanath, there's not even a grain of rice at home. And as for fish or lentils, we haven't seen those for a week now. You must loan me five rupees.'

'Haradhan*da*, how can we manage, if you keep on like this?'

'Shh, don't let the others hear you. Do you want us to starve in front of you all?'

'Why don't your children do something? They are grown up.'

'But the two boys haven't yet been able to land a job. And one of them did finish high school and passed the final exams.'

'All right, but your daughter has a job of some sort.'

'She won't give a penny to her father. You know what this generation is like. She says that she's still an apprentice, that she doesn't get paid yet. It's only Kartik who somehow manages to get hold of five or ten rupees from time to time. But we won't have anything to eat today.'

'I refuse to give you any money. I'll send you some rice and lentils from home.'

'Oh no, no. How can you say that? It's impossible. What will everybody in the colony think? That I am taking a hand-out of rice from you. No, you give me five rupees, and I shall repay you.'

'Why should it be a hand-out? People borrow food from others in times of need.'

'No, one should never take a loan of rice. I can't do it. No one in my family has ever done that.'

For an instant, Biswanath's thoughts went back in time. When they had lived in the village, Haradhan Ray used to observe the Durga Puja festival with a good deal of splendour. On the second day of the Puja, the whole village would be invited to eat at his home. Haradhan himself would serve the guests. He would force food on them, saying, 'Come on, have a couple more of these sweets. You are young yet. This is the time to eat well. And all these are offerings to the goddess. That can never make you sick.'

But even though his heart softened for a while, Biswanath hardened it again. He spoke almost in a tone of reprimand.

'I shall never give you money. As soon as Saturday comes round, you need money. And as soon as you get it, you go over to the bookies to bet on the races. I don't know how you got this addiction for racing Haradhan*da*. You never knew about these things in the village. These are habits for rich people. Not for poor people like us.'

Haradhan protested in low, bitter tones.

'What! I go racing! Who told you? If you can't give me a loan, don't. That doesn't mean you have to ruin my reputation.'

'You think I don't know what's going on? Aren't you always sniffing around that Gobinda from Ghughu-danga?'

'Shhh, quietly, quietly. Why must you shout so? Please give me five rupees today. It's for the last time.'

'You think you can turn your luck by gambling? Does that ever happen to poor people? You would be far better off if you tried to look for some work. You could at least have opened a little shop.'

'Don't you need capital to open a shop? Who's to provide the capital? Will you? Come on then, give me a hundred rupees, and I shall open a cigarette shop.'

'Ha! And you'll be the one who will smoke all the cigarettes in that shop.'

Shashadhar, meanwhile, was still vociferously arguing his point.

'I tell you, I've seen it with my own two eyes. Arjun and that rich man's daughter. You'll see. Those people will bring Arjun home in their car.'

'Why should they?' said Dibya. 'Can't we bring our own boy home? I am sure Haranda will let us use his taxi if we ask him.'

'Listen, he will be brought back in state in a private car. He doesn't need your taxi!'

IV

There used to be a beautiful driveway leading from the road into the colony. But now it was a rough-hewn surface with exposed brickwork. A white car drove straight up this to the dance hall and stopped. A group of children came rushing up and surrounded the car. Women peered from behind the windows, the men stood some way off and watched. A car like this had never come inside the colony before.

The shining new car looked totally out of place among the decrepit habitations, with their shabby inmates. The people sitting inside the car were different too, well-formed, clean people, as if from a different world.

Abanish sat next to the uniformed chauffeur. On the back seat were Probal and Shukla, with Arjun between them. He still had a heavy bandage round his head. Probal gripped one arm, and Abanish quickly came out to hold the other. But Arjun smiled and said, 'No, really, it's all right. You don't have to hold me. I can manage on my own. I really can.'

He was coming home after twelve days. The first couple of days in the hospital were critical. But now he could climb the stairs himself. He had lost a bit of weight over the last few days but his eyes gleamed with the unquenchable fire of life.

He let go his friends' hands, and stood up straight. He turned his head and looked around. The same old surroundings, the same people—but somehow they looked different. Perhaps that always happened when you came back from the nearness of death. It is a very special happiness to return home after a long absence.

Shantilata stood on the front porch, Labonya a bit further back, near the door. Shantilata's face had the expressionless look of a graven statue, her eyes absolutely still. The question she had managed to put aside for a few days, was hammering in her brain again—who could have been cruel and heartless enough to have injured her precious son? Suppose he had died? Her son had never harmed anyone. Nor had she. Oh God, how much more will you make me suffer?

But Arjun's voice was vibrant with life.

'Hello mother, how are you? Hello there Labi, everything all right with you?'

The old dog came running, threw himself at Arjun's feet, turned a somersault and whined his happiness. Arjun patted it on the head, saying, 'Well, Becharam, still alive and kicking I see.'

Then he turned to his companions.

'Abanishda, please come this way. Come Shukla, come Probal. Abanishda, this is my mother. Mother, you know Abanishda, our professor. And this is Shukla and this is Probal—my friends.'

Abanish and Probal folded their hands and bowed to Shantilata. But Shukla bent and touched her feet. This shook Shantilata out of her trance. She quickly took hold of Shukla's hand saying, 'Come inside, my dear, come in and sit down.'

Abanish tried to avoid a visit at this point.

'No, I don't think we'll stay now. We have to go. Arjun, you should go in and rest.'

'Rubbish, you can't leave just now. You have to come in for a little while. Abanishda, please come and have a cup of tea. Come in Probal.'

Abanish had to give in.

'Very well,' he said. 'We'll come. But you don't have to get so excited. Go and lie down. You shouldn't let him get up for a week,' he continued, turning to Shantilata. 'Doctor's instructions. I'll send a medical assistant from our house, who'll change his dressings every day.'

There was only one chair in Arjun's room. Abanish was made to sit on it. Shukla sat on the bed. Probal was the well-dressed one. He always walked carefully, and he had not said a word till now. He would not sit on the bed. He was about to lean against the table, when some awareness of imaginary dust, made him straighten up and keep standing. But Arjun had to lie down at their insistence.

Shukla had been looking around Arjun's room during these exchanges. A room built originally for bygone generations of luxury-loving people, wide walls and high ceilings; the prisms from the chandelier were mostly gone, but you could still see how it had been. The room had not been painted for the last fifteen years, the plaster was falling off in places. There was hardly anything in the room other than Arjun's pile of books. There was not even a bookshelf, the books had just been stacked here and there. Abanish was a born bibliophile, he could never resist books. He started pulling them out and looking through them.

The dog had come inside, and was frisking around, which made Probal a bit wary.

'Don't worry,' said Arjun. 'He won't bite you. He is a most harmless creature. Becharam, get out of here.'

'Where on earth did you find this strange mongrel?' asked Probal, 'I've never seen anybody keep a pet like this.'

'Oh, this one was a great favourite of my brother's. That's why I keep him. I don't remember when he took up with my brother. He is ancient now, look how his hair's falling off. But he still doesn't show any signs of dying. I can't possibly shoo him away.'

'You have certainly chosen a most appropriate name for him,' said Shukla. 'Becharam. It's really very sweet.'

'Yes,' said Abanish, 'you are absolutely right. His name suits his appearance perfectly.'

'Wait, you don't know how harmless he is. Life is sacred to him, so he won't bite anybody. Not only that, he is scared of cats and mice. And we can't afford to give him meat very often. So he's quite happy to have potatoes, aubergines, greens and things like that.'

Abanish got up and looked out of the window.

'Is this where you were sitting when you were hit? Near this window?'

'Please Abanishda, let's not talk about it.'

'What do you mean, not talk about it? You must be very careful from now on. You must never open this window after dark. I am going to tell your mother to see to it.'

'But that's the only window in my room. If I don't open it, I shall suffocate with the heat.'

That was when the guests realized that there was no fan in this room. Immediately they started feeling hot. But Abanish insisted again.

'Never mind the heat. You just have to be very careful, Arjun. At least until the culprit has been caught. My father has telephoned the police, they will send another man to talk to you.'

'But it's been so many days already. What good is talking now?'

'Listen, it's always better to know the enemy. There's less reason to fear then. But an unknown assailant, who comes stealthily in the dark and hits you is...'

'Don't be so scared Abanishda. I'll survive, that's for sure. I won't die so easily.'

'How can you be so sure?' asked Shukla. 'Do you think you are immortal or invulnerable?'

'No, of course not. But I have had many other opportunities to die before this. Since I have survived those, I don't suppose I'll die so easily.'

Labonya and Shantilata came in with some tea and some food. Shantilata still felt tongue-tied in front of strangers. This young man Abanish and his father had made all the arrangements for Arjun's treatment. She wanted to express her gratitude but couldn't find the words. She looked at them with tenderness. What good looking young people, how wealthy too, and yet with not a vestige of pride.

Their neighbours, Haran's wife, mother and children, all came and looked in on Arjun. Other members of the colony also came and went. While visiting Arjun, they made sure they took a good look at Shukla. Shukla was dressed in a white silk sari, her face totally free of embarrassment, her skin smooth, her health radiant, her breasts beautiful—nobody here had seen such loveliness except on the screen. Not only that, here was a young, unmarried girl, and yet she was so totally self-possessed. That was what impressed them most.

'How many families do you have living here now?' asked Abanish.

'Well, originally there were thirty-seven. One of them later moved to Kharagpur with a job. However, our numbers have increased a lot over the last few years, and it's becoming difficult to find room for all of us.'

'I've never been in a place like this. Probal, come with me. Let's go out and have a look around.'

Probal did not feel too enthusiastic about this.

'Why don't we do that some other time?' he suggested. 'Let us allow Arjun to get some rest today. We can come back again.'

'But Arjun doesn't have to come with us.'

At this point Dibya looked in from outside the window.

'Hello, Arjun. How are you feeling now?'

'Fine. How are things with you?'

The fact that Arjun had come back home from the hospital in the car with that same rich man's daughter who had previously been the object of much discussion, was no cause for grievance today. For Haran had announced in the morning that he had to make a trip to Ranaghat, so his taxi would not be available. Besides, there was a fringe benefit to Arjun's ride in the rich man's car. The man's daughter could be looked at. Dibya certainly looked his fill. Shashadhar stood next to him and nudged him to convey that this was the same girl he had been talking about.

'Dibya', said Arjun, 'can you do me a favour? This is our professor, Abanishda. He wants to take a look around the colony. Will you take him around?'

Dibya agreed with enthusiasm. But Shukla, when she got to the door, said to her brother, 'Why don't you go and take a look? I'll just sit here. Don't be too long.'

She had suddenly realized that as soon as she stepped out, hundreds of pairs of eyes would follow her, and that thought made her uneasy. Dibya looked rather crest-fallen.

The Bihari chauffeur stood by the car, twirling his moustache in majestic style. A group of children stood and watched him from a safe distance. Some had even come up to the car and were running their hands all over, almost with affection. The light coating of dust on the car began to bear a pattern of fingerprints. When Abanish stepped out, Dibya tried to warn him about possible disappointment.

'There isn't much to see here, Sir. Just a few huts, like pigsties, and that's where poor people like us huddle together.'

Abanish smiled at him.

'You say you are poor, but your physique is magnificent,' he said to Dibya. 'If I could have had health like yours, I would have no complaints about poverty.'

Finally Shukla could pull the chair up and sit down.

'I can smell that lovely perfume of yours again,' said Arjun. 'It really cheers me up.'

'It's much too hot in here,' said Shukla. 'Can't you buy a fan? How can you work in this heat?'

'Buy a fan. We can't afford such luxuries.'

'Oh, shut up. Stop parading your poverty all the time. I hate it. You know very well you can afford to buy just one fan. It is not such a luxury either—it's a necessity. We have two or three table fans just lying around at home. Shall I send you one of those?'

'No, thank you. You don't have to be that generous. I can manage quite well without a fan.'

'Oh, I see. It will hurt your pride to take a fan from our house. Well, go and buy one then.'

'Yes, I suppose I can afford to buy a fan, just about one. But it doesn't look nice. Nobody else in the colony has a fan in their homes. A fan only in our house...'

'But why do you have to keep on living here? There's only the two of you, your mother and yourself. You can easily rent a flat somewhere else.'

'Yes, we can. But all of us have come through many trials together. How can we just leave the others behind?'

'Stop whining about your sorrows. People should forget such things and try to change their lives.'

'Why are you being so sharp with me today?'

'Just because I feel like it.'

93

Arjun propped himself up on the pillows and raised his head.

'Yes,' he mused, 'we can leave this place, certainly we can. But why? To please whom? I can renounce the scholarship and go find myself a job. I know a lot of people just can't get jobs, but I am sure I shall. I could even become a civil servant.'

'There's no need to brag about yourself to me, you know.'

'I am not bragging. I know the ones who go and qualify for the civil service. Most of them have far worse academic records than mine.'

'It is not enough to have a good academic record. You also have to be smart. Look at Probal. He doesn't have a First, like you do. But he has landed a big, fat job.'

'I know. But I just am not interested in such things. Look at your own brother. Your father is such a well-known doctor. It would have been natural for the son to be the same. He could easily have gone abroad too. But Abanishda just doesn't want any of those things. He is quite happy to be with his books. He is my ideal. I want to be like him.'

'No wonder there's such an understanding between teacher and student. But just remember one thing. Your teacher has a wealthy father. He can afford to make such choices. You are not in his position. You must also think about your mother.'

'Don't keep harping on your family being so wealthy. How much money do they have anyway? Don't you find this kind of pride vulgar?'

Shukla burst into laughter. Then she stopped suddenly.

'Look at me,' she said, 'sitting here with you. I should have gone into the next room and talked with your mother.'

There was the sound of many voices from the next room.

'My mother,' said Arjun, 'is very shy. Even if you had gone to her, she would not have been able to say much. Besides, she would have been a bit apprehensive about talking to you. Whether you would be put off by something or not.'

'That's right. These strange girls from West Bengal. Who knows what quirks they have in their personality!'

'Yes. You just keep sitting here. I never get a chance to see you alone.'

'Go ahead and look at me then. Which way do you want me to turn my head? Towards you or towards the window?'

Arjun did not answer. Shukla was sitting straight in her chair, looking into his eyes. She was slightly taller than the average Bengali girl, her body perfectly formed. Shukla had been the inter-collegiate champion in table tennis. Her movements were fluid and graceful. Had she been born a thousand years ago, she would have looked superb in the costume of a court dancer. Her make-up was done so carefully, that you could see no traces of it. It was impossible to decide if she had touched up her eyes or eyebrows with a *kohl* pencil. And as for the faint tinge of colour in her lips and cheeks, it could well have been natural. Arjun had never touched her to find out. Thick strands of long hair fell unconfined down her back. In her stance and in her look, there was a distinct element of pride. But whenever she put on this look of pride, there was inevitably a sparkle of laughter in her eyes and about her mouth. Obviously she enjoyed the pose.

This young woman could definitely be described as beautiful. The sight of her did your eyes good. But there is also an awareness of pain in the consciousness of beauty. Arjun felt a strange feeling of loss for no reason.

He did not get to see her very often. She had numerous friends, and she was always occupied with them. Arjun would run into her occasionally, when he was visiting Abanish. But there was never much conversation between them. And there was nothing romantic about the fact that Shukla addressed Arjun by the familiar *tumi*. Shukla was a person who had no self-consciousness. She used *tumi* with many people. In the set she belonged to, it was usual for boys and girls to use *tumi* among themselves casually. To descend from the formaility of *apni* into the familiarity of *tumi* did not require an exchange of notes, or secret, romantic encounters.

'Haven't you had enough?'

'No.'

'Then you must start contemplating me in meditation. I have to go now.'

'I have better things to do than meditate on you.'

'That's right. On the contrary, you should meditate on the goddess Saraswati. That will be good for your thesis.'

'Why did you never come to the hospital again, after that first visit of yours? And even today, you didn't come upstairs to the ward.'

'Did I give you an undertaking to visit every day?'

'No, no, it's not a question of an undertaking.'

'You obviously think I have nothing else to do, than going and spending time in the hospital.'

'Of course not. I know you must be very busy.'

'Well, who asked you to get into trouble and break your head?'

'That was a piece of good luck, wasn't it? That was why you came to see me. It's impossible to see you alone.'

As if this was the funniest thing she had ever heard, Shukla started heaving with laughter.

'Does that mean you broke your head intentionally?' she asked. 'Why did you never tell me before that you were dying to see me alone?'

Arjun did not reply. He had nearly started to scratch his head, when his fingers encountered the bandage. The accumulated irritation of so many days in his head was unbearable. He just could not make anybody understand that. When the man came tomorrow to change his dressing, he must remember to scratch his head properly.

Shukla got up from her chair.

'How big is this colony of yours? When will my brother get back?'

'Sit down. They will be back soon enough. Why are you fidgeting like this?'

'Please. Can't I make you understand that I have other things to do? I can't just sit here all day.'

'What other things? There are no classes now.'

'Can't I have anything to do but attend class?'

'No, you can't. I refuse to believe you do anything else.'

'But I have to be somewhere.'

'Where?'

'I am supposed to go to a film. I'll be late.'

'Who are you going with?'

'Barun went and got the tickets. Barun, Probal and I.'

'A fine life you lead! Going to films and wandering around.'

Shukla smiled.

'What else is there to do? Tell me.'

'Sure, what else? Girls can have nothing better to do than seeing films and gadding about.'

'But do you expect me to bury myself in my books, like you? Or should I go into the kitchen and meddle with pots and pans?'

'Ah, I see I have made a mistake. It's hard for me to define areas of work for women.'

Even now, there was the touch of a smile about Shukla's mouth. Her bright eyes looked at Arjun. Her father was a successful doctor, who just kept on earning money. He never had a free moment to himself. Shukla had never known want from her childhood. Nature had been generous with her too. She had beauty and health as well as intelligence. Her academic career was not too bad, and she was a good sportswoman. What was there for a girl like this to do, except to enjoy life? And yet there had to be something. It was just that Arjun could not figure it out right now.

'How are you Arjun? I thought I'd come and see you.'

It was Grandfather Nishi, holding Labonya by the hand. Arjun quickly sat up on his bed. Grandfather still had not managed to forget the verb 'see'. His blind eyes were always glistening with moisture, but he had come to 'see' Arjun. Shukla went and stood to one side of the bed. Grandfather let go of Labonya's hand and moved forward, guessing his way.

'Please come in, Grandfather,' said Arjun. 'I am quite well. How have you been yourself?'

Grandfather stretched his arm out towards Arjun, but touched Shukla instead. Grandfather's trembling hand with its swollen veins fell on Shukla's smooth, rounded arm. He understood immediately, and said, 'Who is this girl?'

'My professor's sister. They brought me home today in their car.'

'Good, very good. Bless you, my dear. It is only because of the help given by people like you that this boy of ours has done so well. His mother has suffered a lot you know, all her life she has suffered. Such a precious boy. I can't imagine who could have hurt him so. How could anybody be so ruthless?'

Arjun tried to overcome his embarrassment by cutting in.

'You know, Shukla, Grandfather was a revolutionary during the days of the British. He lost his eyes because of torture at the hands of the police. He could even use a revolver.'

Labonya had been standing in one corner of the room during this interchange. She was looking at Shukla out of the corner of her eye. Labonya was dressed in an ordinary printed cotton sari, and a torn blouse, but she was determined not to let Shukla see the tear, so she kept standing sideways. As soon as her eyes met Shukla's, Labonya pointed to the chair and said, 'Why don't you sit down? You don't have to keep standing.'

There was no trace of the haughty, imperious look on Shukla's face now. That was a face she reserved only for men. Now she looked very soft and modest, as she spoke to Labonya.

'Why don't you sit down yourself?'

'Oh no, please. It's all right for me. I am as good as a member of this household.'

But Shukla did not sit down. Instead she moved closer towards Labonya and started talking to her once more.

'I haven't met you before. My name is Shukla Mukherjee.'

V

Barun had once put on a very innocent face and asked me, 'Arjun, your family were *zamindars* in East Bengal, weren't they?'

'No,' I had replied. 'We had nothing to do with *zamindars*, landlords and their like. We were just as poor in East Bengal.'

Barun's amazement had been obvious.

'How strange. I have heard that all the refugees who came from East Bengal had belonged to the landed aristocracy. They all gorged themselves on milk and butter, and honey too. It's only here that they have such a rotten life.'

He had been joking, of course. It was true that many people made up stories about their past. A lot of them came to India and gave inflated descriptions of their property in East Bengal. It was only human nature to magnify the past. But it was equally true that most of us had had a little bit of land there. That was why the epithet of 'refugee', and being known as landless, was so humiliating to us. There was not much by the way of industry, in the days before Pakistan. Life centred round agriculture. Land was everything, which was why there was still an attachment to land. After the creation of Pakistan, of course, there was quick progress in road building and the setting up of factories. But the Hindus never got to feel any sense of belonging or identification with all that. Perhaps only the blacks in America have understood and continue to understand how hateful it is to be second class citizens—and even they have now managed to acquire some equality of status.

My own family had possessed land too—five *bighas* of land. Not that I ever got to see where that land was. But once a year, a respectably dressed Muslim gentleman would come to see my father, and pay him his dues. We knew he had rented that land from us. Of course, he did not cultivate the land with his hands. He employed others for that. But at the end of the year, he would pay us the revenue. This was a memory of early childhood. I never saw him again when I was a bit older.

By any standards, we are better off here than we ever were in our home in East Bengal. There is no doubt about that. There we had never lived in concrete houses. Our walls were made of mud, and we invariably suffered during the monsoon. On top of that, there were the depredations of sneak thieves and burglars. They would use a shovel and cut through the earthen walls and foundations, and come inside.

I still have not forgotten my first memory of seeing a burglar when I was a child. We usually left the lantern on all night. In the middle of the night, by the dim glow of the lantern, I saw a man in our room, his dark body gleaming. Later I heard they usually oiled themselves before coming. He was fumbling in the alcove on our wall. I was about six years old at that time. On one side lay my brother, on the other, my mother. My throat went completely dry. From the next room, I could hear my father's snoring. I knew that I was the only one awake. That poor thief, he could not have found much to steal in our house.

Finally, he started pulling off the blanket covering the three of us. He was only about three feet away from me; I could smell the rancid oil on his body—and I kept on staring at him with my eyes wide open. Before this, I had always thought of thieves as a different species, we had heard such strange stories about them. But this one was just a man, he looked like a man.

When the blanket was finally pulled off, I could not bear the winter cold. I turned on my side, and screamed, 'Mother!' But my mother immediately gripped my hand hard and said, 'Quiet!' That meant that she too had been awake. But she was afraid that if we confronted the thief he would have had no hesitation in plunging a dagger into us.

We waited for quite some time after the thief left, before calling my father and raising an outcry. At that age, what brought tears to my eyes was the realization of the thief's cruelty. Even on a winter night, he had had no compunction about robbing a child of its blanket.

A couple of days later I saw one of the boys in our village wearing my thick yellow cotton vest. That had also been stolen that night. It was not a new one, for my father had bought it for me a year-and-a-half ago. But it was such a favourite of mine, that I hardly ever wore it except on special occasions. Most of the time we wore loose tops, sewn at home by my mother. So even a vest or a shirt was quite special. When I saw my vest on that boy, I ran home to tell my mother. But she just told me not to talk about it to anybody. No, we had no right to complain, certainly not in the hearing of others, because we were a minority. No outsider can understand the oppressive hurt of that feeling. There is such a rot in our civilization that we now judge men by the strength of their numbers.

A mud house was not our only problem. Food was another and it stayed with us round the year. My father, as it happened, was never particularly interested in his job. On top of that, his salary was not paid regularly by the school. I had not yet been born during the Bengal famine of 1943, but my brother used to tell me how they had lived for day after day on boiled sweet potatoes. On alternate days, there would be a liquid concoction of rice—and that was almost a feast. As for things like milk and butter—they were rare indeed.

Fish we did have. But then, if my brother and I brought home too many from the pond or the canal, my mother would get angry. You need oil to cook fish in, how was she to get hold of so much oil? So even catching a lot of fish was an offence. And since we were Brahmins, we could not possibly sell the extra fish, we had to give it away. The one strange thing I remember is that every time I went out fishing, I was sure to wet my bed at night. People say that if you go to bed in the same clothes you wear while fishing, this is bound to happen. But the funny part of it was that I would dream of feeling the urge to piss, of getting out of bed, opening the door and sitting down next to the gutter outside the house and actually peeing—then, in the middle of the dream, I would wake up feeling the wet bedclothes, and my mother would let me have it.

Sometimes Jainuddin would stop by our house on his way back from the market and ask my mother, 'There's an extra jug of milk today, do you want it madam?'

Mother would say, 'I don't have any money. But there is a fair-sized gourd, if you can take that in exchange...'

*

Yes, certainly, I am better off in comparison to those days. So what is there to feel sorry about? If there had been no Pakistan, if we had stayed on in the village, then all I would have been by now would be a teacher in the village school. Could I have hoped for more? How would I have had the opportunity of higher education? My father could not even buy all my school books! Or suppose, I had managed to receive a scholarship and gone on to get a job in some big city like Calcutta or Delhi. Would I then have gone back to the village, ever? Come now, Arjun, let us have the truth. Are you so attached to the village that you would have gone back there voluntarily, after acquiring all the advantages of an urban life? At the most, you would have returned for two or three years, to enjoy the beauties of rural Bengal. Or perhaps like so many others, you would have made annual visits during the Pujas. Or been like Uncle Naresh who worked in the navy and wandered around all over the world—but then would come home every two or three years and say, 'Whatever you may say, there's no pleasure greater than living at home.'

No, the regret lies in the fact that we can never go back, that we were forced to leave our home. And that is heart-breaking.

In history you read about many races leaving one country and going to another. Even the Aryans came from West Asia, but they are not sighing regretfully for

West Asia anymore. The Irish who emigrated to settle in the States don't mourn for Ireland any longer. Look at the whites in Australia, none of them belonged there originally. And even the Indian settlers in the West Indies, or in Mauritius, do not wish to return to India. But you cannot compare their lot with ours. They have acquired rights. It is hard enough to forget the sorrow of forcible eviction and not being able to return. Over and above, there is another sorrow, that of having been treated like beggars and destitutes here. No one showed us any kinship, any closeness.

Though I was offered more substantial scholarships from other colleges, I still chose to enrol in Presidency College. But frequently after that, I used to feel I had made a mistake. For quite a few months I felt thoroughly awkward, I could not speak freely with anybody. My clothes were shabby, an ironed shirt unthinkable in those days; the straps on my sandal kept breaking and the whole thing was so studded with nails, that there was always one raised nail hurting my foot. The students in my class were mostly bright-faced, well-dressed boys and girls. They had a lot of fun and games between them—but I was the perpetual outsider. Many of them knew me because I had had a place in the school-leaving exams, but I could never be one of them.

A lot of the boys used to smoke in the college grounds. A packet of cigarettes in those days cost one rupee, or even more, one stick could not have been less than ten paise—then the bell would ring for classes, or one of the professors would be seen coming and immediately they would throw away the cigarette after two or three puffs. The sight upset me. That was a time when I would constantly put my hand into my pocket and count my change; five or ten paise meant a lot to me. None of those boys had any idea of the things I had had to do. On my way out of East Bengal, I had begged for food, once in the colony I had worked as a waiter in the teashop. If any customer tipped me five or ten paise in those days, I would think of him as a god.

So many things have changed now. But in those early days at college, surrounded by those well-fed, well-dressed young people, I could never escape the feeling that I did not belong with them. I was the immigrant, and I could not fit in. Their preoccupations were different, the sound of their laughter different. Even while I sat in class, my thoughts went back to my mother who made clothes for other people, to my brother who was crazy and who could get into trouble any time—a constant apprehension of the ground being pulled from under my feet.

Dipankar was the boy who had stood first in the final school-leaving examinations. Eleven points ahead of me in the total score. A big difference. Naturally, I envied him. Or maybe it was not envy, just resentment. Not that Dipankar had the least hint of superiority in his manner. He was a very sweet-natured person. He lives now in England. I went to his house several times. A huge house on Keyatola Road, where even the servants were better off than I was. Dipankar had his own study. He could buy any book he wanted. He certainly was intelligent, but he also had two professors to tutor him at home. Why should I not be resentful? I could have scored those eleven points too. But I had to leave my books every night and wander all over the place to search for my poor brother and bring him home. So I would say to myself, 'All right Dipankar, you just wait. Next time I'll beat you, that's for sure. If I can't get you down in the BSc exams, I'm not worth anything.' These were my weapons, these were what would give me the mastery. I could not lose, I would not lose, I had to win...

*

'Is that you Labi? Come in. Switch the light on.'

'How are you getting on Arjunda? I hope you haven't had a temperature today.'

'No, no. I am fine, really I am. No more dressing for the wound from tomorrow. And day after tomorrow, I shall go out. I must go to the college once.'

'That wound will leave a scar on your neck won't it?'

'So what? Listen, are you working hard? The exams are not too far off, you know.'

'Yes, and just look at you. I was hoping to get some help from you these last few days. But you had to go and break your head just now.'

'Well, why don't you bring your books along and tell me what you need help with? I may have broken my head, but my brains are still intact. I can help you.'

'Indeed. And what will your mother say? How can I impose on you now, in the state you are in?'

'Bring them tomorrow, then. I tell you, it will be all right.'

'No, I won't come tomorrow. I won't come to your house again, ever. I won't even speak to you.'

'Why, what's the matter? What have I done?'

'You never bothered to introduce me to your friend Shukla.'

'What do you mean, introduce? I saw you two talking away.'

'Yes, but that was only because she came forward and spoke to me. You introduced her to everybody except me. Why, don't you think I am human?'

'My God, where have you picked up all these notions of formalities? Girls can always go and speak to other girls. There's nothing more to it.'

'She's a great friend of yours, isn't she Arjunda?'

'Shukla? No, I wouldn't call her a very intimate friend. We just know each other a bit. She has many friends.'

'Well, she's very smart, isn't she? And though she comes from a wealthy family, there isn't the least touch of pride about her.'

'No pride? You must be joking. I know, she must have put on her most sincere manner with you. Just remember, that is also a pose with them.'

'I don't know about that, but I really liked her. And so beautiful too, just like Hema Malini.'

'Oh, I see, that's what you have been doing. Watching Hindi films and getting to know the faces of film-stars.'

'Certainly not. Who's going to take me to the movies?'

'You don't need someone to take you. All you have to do is buy a ticket and walk in.'

'All by myself? Nobody goes to see a film alone. You really don't know anything. Have you ever gone to a film by yourself?'

'When have I ever been to see a film? Uttam Kumar, Suchitra Sen—all these film-stars are just names to me. I have never seen them.'

'You mean to say, you haven't been to a single film in all this time?'

'No, I suppose I did get to see a couple when I was in college. One was a picture called *Raikamal*. There was an actress called Kaberi Bose in it, I remember.'

'You really are something! That was an ancient film. It does no harm to go to the pictures occasionally. All you do night and day is sit here poring over your books.'

'Labonya, there's someone calling you from outside.'

'Let him. That disgusting Sukhen keeps on pestering me. You get well first, then you can tell them off. They are really getting to be unbearable.'

'Why should they pay any attention to me?'

'You are the only person they are somewhat scared of. Everybody else is considered of no account. Our colony has become such an ugly place now. Squabbles and fights all the time. Besides the boys have become so crude...'

'It's not their fault. They can't get any jobs. Just look at them—young fellows must have something to do.'

'Do they have to be so vulgar just because they are unemployed?'

'You won't understand. It is all very complicated.'

'Oh well, I don't suppose you care one bit. You will soon get a good job somewhere and go away. But for us, we have to stay and rot in this hell for the rest of our lives.'

'My dear, you will go away too, when you get married.'

'Yes, and where to? Just another place like this. Otherwise I'll have to become like Purnima.'

'Purnima? Oh yes, what does she do? I believe she has a job of some sort.'

'Never mind Purnima. It was such a pleasure to talk to Shukladi the other day.'

'What, she has already become your sister, has she?'

'They seem like beings from another world, don't they? God has given them everything. It is only people like us who have nothing but bad luck.'

'Now then, Labonya, don't be so envious. What good will that do? Perhaps one day you will also be as fortunate as they are.'

'I can gain a fortune in a lottery, but will I be as beautiful as Shukla? You know something, people who have been wealthy for generations have wonderful looks as well.'

'What have you got to complain about? You are a good-looking girl yourself. Doesn't everybody say so? I think you are very pretty. A fair complexion is not the only attribute of beauty.'

'Nonsense. I know very well what I do look like. Didn't you say Shukla*di* has a lot of friends? Well, I'll tell you one thing. I don't have a single friend. Everybody wants to tear me apart, and devour me. They are determined to corrupt me. You are smiling Arjun*da*. You just live in your books, you understand nothing. You have no idea how difficult it is for a girl coming from a family like mine, to keep herself unspoilt.'

'All right, stop whining. You'd better run off now. Somebody is really calling you. It's probably your mother.'

*

I had tutored Shukla at home for a few days only. She did not want to continue it. Just as well. But I kept going to their house quite often. I would not have been able to carry on with my research if Abanish*da* had not helped me so much. I have been really fortunate to have received affection from a man like him.

Abanish*da*'s house was always full of people. A constant flow of visitors coming and going, a pervasive uproar. The two front rooms were waiting rooms for the patients coming to see Abanish*da*'s father, and they were always crowded. Abanish*da* had four other brothers and three sisters. Their friends went straight upstairs when they came. Everyone had his or her own room. Apart from friends, there were also the relatives who kept coming and going. It was impossible to know how many people sat down to a meal in that house every day. The family was not too worried about thefts either, Or perhaps little things were always getting stolen—it was just that nobody cared much.

At one time I was under the impression that rich men's children always came to a bad end because they had so much of everything, possessions and opportunities. But it was not like that at all in Abanish*da's* family. Their father never had time to find out what they were doing, and yet all the children did well in their studies, all of them were well brought up and intelligent. They had plenty of opportunity to mix with the opposite sex, and yet there was not a hint of scandal about any of them. I suppose in one sense, it was a remarkable phenomenon. It's never like that in fiction.

But none of the brothers or sisters was as reckless as Shukla. Every time I went to that house, her room was full of friends. Often, they were all going off on a picnic, or to a film. Invitations to parties were just as common. I don't know how she managed to find time for her studies in that mad whirl of socializing. But she always did well. Shukla was a person I had never seen alone. Abanish*da* said to me one day with a smile, 'Do you know why Shukla refused to be tutored by you? She thinks her boy-friends will be jealous or feel hurt, if they see a young man as her tutor.'

There is a dart board in Shukla's room. A square board, made of soft wood, hung up on the wall. There are several coloured circles in the middle of the board. The game consists of trying to hit the bulls-eye with small arrows or darts. Shukla would listen to Western music on her record player, and keep throwing darts, one after the other. Sort of like hitting a bulls-eye with a javelin. That was the kind of stylish game Shukla preferred. Many of her friends also had a go at it, but I never saw anybody hit the centre. Shukla once said to me, 'Arjun, you give it a try. Let us see if you can hit something. I have heard that people from East Bengal can be very deft.'

I refused to try. For fear of failing. I never took part in a game where I could lose, without being adequately prepared for it. If I ever see Shukla alone in her room, I may try.

She has a friend called Akhtar. At one time I used to think that it was Akhtar she would marry. For there was no prejudice against Muslims in Shukla's family. There would be no opposition to this marriage. Besides, Shukla was such an obstinate girl. It was easy to see that opposition would never stop her from doing something. Akhtar and Shukla looked very well together. There was a lot of similarity in their characters.

I like Akhtar a great deal. He has a bright well-groomed appearance, and he is very pleasant to talk to. He had been to a Westernized school in Ajmer, and he is absolutely fluent in English. His family own two or three tea estates in Jalpaiguri, as well as having a lot of business in the transport sector. They are enormously wealthy. And no one could be more suited to a life of fun than Akhtar.

Whenever I've met Akhtar, I've felt the Muslims in India not have to labour under any unease or discrimination. He comes and goes in Shukla's house just as he pleases, says whatever comes into his head. He is also a bit strong-willed, so he can really tell you off, when he loses his temper. He frequently goes touring all over India in his car. It did not seem that being a Muslim cramps his style at all. Later, much later, I realized my mistake, when I met Mizanur. Akhtar comes from a wealthy family. The rich never have problems in any country. It is only the poor who suffer.

I had to tutor a boy called Badal who was doing his BSc degree. He lived in Park Circus. One day he told me that a friend of his would also like to have some assistance from me. But the boy was very poor, he would not be able to pay me anything. So Badal brought Mizanur to me. Mizanur's family lived in a slum. His father had a minor job in a tannery. Their family was numerous. This boy, Mizanur, was desperately trying to complete his education and become self-sufficient. In the riots of 1964, one of his elder brothers had been killed. He had left behind a wife and three children.

There was an unmistakable look on Mizanur's face. The oily look of fear. In my childhood in East Bengal, I had seen this self-same look on the faces of all my relatives and neighbours. I am sure I had had it too. The humiliation of being in a minority. The mortification of not being a part of things. If a crowd ever gathered on the street to beat up a pickpocket, Mizanur would never hang around there. Scared, he would disappear. Just as I could never complain to anyone about the theft of my yellow vest, of my harmonica.

Mizanur kept reminding me of my childhood. I really did want to talk to him freely, frankly. To try and find a way out of his problem with him. Mizanur may have been a Muslim, but he did not have to be a second-class citizen in India. He was entitled to every opportunity under the law. But all this could not take away his sense of constant unease. It was so unfair. Why should he not be able to forget the fact that he was a Muslim, a member of a minority group, and just think of himself as a human being?

I could see that it would not be easy for Mizanur to get a job even after he acquired a BSc degree. He would have to keep looking for opportunities to get to Pakistan. Once there, he would no longer have to belong to a minority. He would be free as a fish in water. It wouldn't surprise me if he broke out in vehement condemnation of India. Perhaps one Muslim in a million could take advantage of the constitution and become the President of India. But the others, the peasants and the workers, definitely laboured under a sense of insecurity. Had I been involved in politics, I would not set my priorities on the acquisition of land for the landless, or on workers' movements. I would first try to abolish religious distinctions among the people of India. That is what is most necessary for them. This problem will have ceased to exist on the day when the people of both East and West Bengal stop thinking of themselves as Hindus or Muslims, but as Bengalis. It is not through religion but through the cohesion of our culture that we remain Bengalis. If you ignore religion and talk about the equality of men, then you are trying to achieve the impossible.

In the early days of my college life, I was also very nervous about going into a restaurant or coffee house. I kept thinking there must be a thousand and one rules of etiquette operating there. If I made one mistake people would snigger at me and call me a country boor. Which hand for the knife and which hand for the fork—that was a big problem for me. But everything has become so easy now. I even know that in big restaurants it is the fashion these days to eat your chicken with your fingers. There is nothing boorish about that.

Towards the end of my time in College, there was a boy called Biman who often invited me out. Not just me, many of us. Biman had a habit of never letting anyone pay if he went to a restaurant with them. He was extraordinarily free with his money. He left magnificent tips for the waiters—two, three, four rupees. Of course, I discovered the reason behind this careless generosity. Biman was also from East Bengal. His family had been landlords in Comilla, and they were quite well off in Calcutta too. Biman had still not acquired the right accent—one or two words in the East Bengali dialect would slip into his speech from time to time. But he allowed no one the opportunity to despise him. He wanted to keep on staggering everybody with his largesse.

One day, in one of these restaurants, a lady in a pair of glasses had kept staring at me for a long time. When I was about to leave with my friends, she suddenly called out to me and asked, 'Aren't you Arjun? Do you recognize me?'

I had not been able to make out who she was, so I stared at her uncomfortably. I had not had too many opportunities to mix with women. And this lady certainly looked unfamiliar. Yet she had started out by using the informal *tumi* right from the start. She looked at me for some more time. Then she spoke again.

'So you don't remember me? You are Arjun, aren't you? When did you all come over here?'

At last, there was no room for mistakes anymore. Those last words told me who she was: Amala*di*'s sister, Kamala*di*. A daughter of the Dutta family in our village. A shiver passed through my body. The grapefruit tree, the canal-side, the deserted banyan tree—they all came before my eyes.

Kamala*di* introduced me to her husband. They were both teaching in colleges. To see a girl from our village so happily settled in Calcutta gave me ineffable happiness.

'You were such a child,' said Kamala*di*, 'when I saw you last. Now you have grown up, and you look so good, so well got up. How is your brother?'

I could not answer. Tears choked me. My brother was no longer alive, nor was Amala*di*. Many things can be rectified, returned to normalcy. But who will ever redress the balance for those lives lost unnecessarily?

Another incident. Abanish*da's* family owned a house in Naihati. A little way out of Naihati city. A beautiful house, I'd been there twice. There was a huge garden all around, with two guards to keep watch. That was where we once went for a picnic. A whole group. That was when Shukla nearly got drowned while bathing in the pond. But no, I was not going to talk about the picnic. There's another thing to say. We were to take the 5.45 train out of Sealdah. I had said I would meet them at the station, but Abanish*da* would not agree. He picked me up from home.

In the car there were Abanish*da*, his wife Maya, their two children, his younger sisters Tandra and Shukla. The chauffeur was driving and we all had to sit crammed against each other. I was in the front, next to Shukla. She had already had a bath. And so early in the morning, her make-up was at imperceptibly fine as ever; the same nearly invisible touch of *kohl* around the eyes, the perfume on her body. Since her friends were not around, she was engrossed in conversation with me. She was telling me about her horse-riding experiences in Darjeeling.

I was totally immersed in listening to her, even when we got to Sealdah, got out of the car and started walking along with platform. Shukla had not finished her story yet, when a sudden comment of Maya's came to my ears, 'Oh God, look, more refugees.'

I felt as if somebody had hit me straight in the chest. I could feel the blood draining away from my face. I looked around. Hundreds of refugees were lying all over the platform—most of them were from the peasant class. Some had woken up, but many of them were fast asleep. There was one sleeping girl who could have been Amala*di* herself—Amala*di*, whose disfigured corpse had been found in the jute fields. It was as if Amala*di* herself had managed to escape with her life. And yet, I had not even noticed them till now.

There was a time when I too had stayed on the platform, beside my mother. Today, I happened to be so engrossed in listening to a beautiful, young woman, that I had not paid the slightest attention to a group of people who were just like I had been then. They too had had their land and their homes. They too had left everything behind and were lying around like destitute beggars, waiting for charity. I had found shelter, I had managed to survive, and so I could not be bothered to look at these people. And yet we complained about the indifference of the West Bengalis!

That was when I also remembered Subimal*babu*. My friend Dipankar had taken me to his sister's house once. His brother-in-law had built an enormous house in Jodhpur Park. The ostentation there was overpowering. A bit like the houses of film-stars. There were four ashtrays in the living room, but one did not feel like flicking ash into any of them—they were such expensive objects. Subimal*babu* owned an aluminium factory.

One thing surprised me about that household. Everybody spoke with an East Bengal accent. With outsiders, of course, they put on their best Calcutta accents—but at home they spoke their native dialect. To be sure, the dialect did not come out entirely naturally, you felt they were trying to acquire a new language. Subimal's family had severed their links with East Bengal in 1947. They had managed to bring out quite a bit of money, and then they had been very successful in their business in India. But their attachment to the country they had left behind twenty-three years ago, was still tremendous. At every opportunity you heard comments like 'There are so many geniuses among us East Bengalis.' Or, if they heard of a famous Bengali, 'Of course, he comes from our part of the world. He's from Bikrampur.'

When Subimal heard that I was from Faridpur, he nearly rushed over to embrace me. His words came out with extraordinary fervour. 'It's such a pleasure to be able to talk freely with someone from home.'

I, however, could never feel any sense of kinship with Subimal and his family. All through the visit I felt uncomfortable. Perhaps, as a matter of chance, both of us had come from the same district called Faridpur. But we had nothing in common.

At one point Subimal said sadly, 'This partition has done a lot of harm to the culture and language of Bengal.' And then, he again started getting quite militant.

'Yes it was a good thing that Pakistan came about. Those Hindus in East Bengal oppressed the Muslims terribly. They never gave them a chance for education, or for getting good jobs. Coming into physical contact with a Muslim was considered a sin, you couldn't even accept a glass of water from the hands of a Muslim. Isn't it only just, to reap the harvest of that kind of inhumanity? And look at the Muslims there now. Look at the wonderful progress they are making. It's their boys who have sacrificed their lives for the Bengali language.' I listened to the whole thing in silence. I could not say a word.

He had also brought up the question of refugees. Those from the Punjab were admirable, and the ones from East Bengal were worthless layabouts—that was the drift of his speech. The Bengalis had not become self-reliant, they had no sense of self-respect. He had also condemned the government and the leaders of the country. A stirring speech for two-and-a-half hours.

But it had left me cold. It had sounded like a speech from a foreigner, not one of us. I was a friend of his brother-in-law, I was a bright student from Presidency College. So he had no objection to embracing me as a fellow countryman. But would he have done the same for those who were lying on the platform at Sealdah station? He was so well-off. Could he not have helped just one refugee family to establish itself? Those people from East Bengal who had made good in West Bengal—had they ever got together in a concerted attempt to help the poor refugees? The Ballygunge and New Alipore areas of Calcutta were full. of wealthy East Bengalis who had never lifted a finger to help their countrymen. All they did was lament the things past, the *hilsa* fish and the date palm molasses, the good things of life. But the people of East Bengal did not exist for them.

Subimal*babu* also said, 'What is so remarkable about West Bengal? Just show me one great river! Whereas we have such wonderful, big rivers in East Bengal. People who live next to rivers inevitably have generous souls. Every time I think of rivers like the Padma or the Meghna, I feel a thrill of excitement. Look, even now the hair is standing up on my body.'

But by then, I had stopped listening to him. My eyes had strayed absently outside. On the balcony Subimal's two children were playing. Two children, like dolls made out of butter. Exquisite complexions, radiant with health, beautiful hair, the smiles on their faces like endowments from the gods. I remembered how we had suffered in our own childhood. The sorrows of children are even more heart-rending than the sorrows of adults. Our childhood, so dear to us, was spent in a lot of misery. I sat there thinking, let these children, at least, not suffer, let them taste the fruits of joy.

VI

Dibya used to have a job at a factory near Ghughudanga. But for the last six months he had been unemployed. There was a lockout at the factory, and there seemed to be no likelihood of its re-opening soon. He had tried to find a job at a few other places, but the job market was very tight.

A vigorous, energetic young man, he felt restless at not having anything to do with his time. Haran, the taxi driver, had made Dibya his assistant for a few days. He needed a companion after eight o'clock in the evening, and a bodyguard like Dibya was invaluable. But Dibya did not like that after a few days. He would have preferred to have learnt driving from Haran. He, too, could have driven a taxi then. But Haran just did not have the time, and Dibya felt nervous about practising with a car that did not belong to him.

He had not done too badly at school. But in the chaos of leaving his homeland and settling down here, he had lost two years. So when he went back to school again, he just could not cope. Though he was older than Arjun, he was admitted with Arjun in the same grade. The shame of failing when Arjun stood first in class, made him quit school and studies. Shortly after that, he had fortuitously happened on the factory job.

Before the last election, he had been sought after by members of several political parties. They had fed him generously, and given him money too. That was when Dibya started to realize that he had a special kind of importance. Now he could enter teashops and have tea without paying for it; stroll over to the cigarette stall and pick out cigarettes just like that; walk into ration shops and demand a kilogram of sugar. If anyone had the temerity to ask him for payment, he would bunch his neck muscles, glare at them and say, 'You'll get your money, all in good time. What's the hurry anyway, eh? What's the rush?' He did not have to say any more.

Dibya had also acquired a group of followers. They were to be seen with him always. These young men would steal light bulbs from the street lamps, cut through the electric lines, even take off the letter boxes attached to house doors—Dibya himself did not descend to such petty larceny, but he did give them protection.

The road was used regularly for smuggling rice. One side of the canal was under statutory rationing, the other was uncontrolled. So rice was brought from one side to the other. At one time the smugglers could get away with small bribes to the police. But now, they had to contend with Dibya. Frequently he would appear in the middle of the road, stop the bicycle-rickshaw or van carrying rice and say in his booming voice, 'Open up. Let's see how much rice you have. Why don't you move, you bastard, you son of a bitch.'

And he would take half of what was there. You could not go and complain to the police about being robbed of smuggled rice, could you? One man once pulled out his knife to stab Dibya. But Dibya wrenched both his arms so badly that he would never be able to raise his arms over his head again. The knife was still with Dibya. Not that he ever needed to use it.

Arjun was putting his books in order, when Dibya asked from outside his window, 'Were you thinking of going out, Arjun?'

'Yes,' said Arjun, 'I thought I might go out today. Why don't you come in?'

'No, I won't, not now. What time do you have to leave?'

'Oh, in about half-an-hour's time. I have to pop in to the university.'

'There was something I wanted to talk to you about.'

'What is it? Tell me. Come inside.'

'No, some other time.'

Arjun discovered a packet of cigarettes among his

books. A bit stale. But that did not matter. He had started smoking just to stay up late and work. But it had never become a habit.

'Would you like a cigarette, Dibya?' he asked.

'Yes, wouldn't mind one.'

As he approached the window to hand over the cigarette, Arjun noticed that Dibya was looking rather glum. Something had made him feel depressed. Dibya felt the iron bars in the window with his powerful hands before speaking again.

'Your chair is quite distant from the window, Arjun. So they had to really reach forward to hit you. How come you never saw them?'

'It was dark. And I was sitting with my back to the window.'

'Strange, very strange.'

'Dibya, have you any idea who it was?'

Dibya raised his lowering face to Arjun's and looked at him. Then in tones of suppressed violence, he said, 'If I knew who it was by now I would have torn him apart.'

Arjun smiled lightly.

'No, no. I am sure that will not be necessary. Whoever it was, he won't be able to harm me again.'

The sight of Arjun's tall figure, his long fingers and sharp, brilliant eyes, did make you want to believe that it was impossible to vanquish him easily face to face. But still Dibya warned him.

'You'd better be careful, Arjun. If these people dare to come inside the colony and do something so outrageous, God knows what they will do if they ever get you outside. Listen, you know that girl, who came to see you the other day. Are you sure her family does not have a grudge against you? Of course, her brother did seem rather nice.'

For some time Arjun just could not stop laughing.

'Shukla's father?' he gasped finally, 'How could you possibly have imagined such a thing? Do you think a girl's father will hire thugs to beat up a boy just because he has spoken to his daughter? You must be crazy.'

'Don't be so sure. These rich Calcutta people. They may be sweet as honey in their words, but at the bottom of their hearts they hate us.'

Arjun threw his cigarette stub out of the window.

'What about Kewal Singh?' he asked. 'Has he made any more trouble?'

'Why should Kewal Singh want to make trouble? He never does anyway. I tell you Arjun, you dislike him for no good reason.'

'No, Dibya. Let me tell you something. That man is up to no good. He's planning something deep and devious. Do you know he goes and meets the Duttas quite regularly?'

'With the Duttas. That's a good one. What can the Duttas do to us? Let them try coming in here and I'll break their necks.'

'That's all you can do, and all you can think about. If only one could get everything by brute force.'

*

The Duttas had been the owners of the property at one time. They had tried to oust the new settlers after they had occupied the place by force. The problem, however, was that you could not openly bring in your henchmen and throw the settlers out. That would lead to open confrontation on a large scale. And the refugees were so desperate, they would hang on to the place for dear life, and just not leave. Besides, in the early days, several of the political parties had shown great sympathy for the refugees, though nothing much had been heard from them since. So the Duttas had hit upon another plan.

As West Bengal's condition started going downhill, so did a lot of the local people begin to feel that it was the refugees who were at the root of the evil. It was they who had made the place a dung-heap, it was because of them that unemployment was such a big problem. The refugees were lazy, unwilling to work hard—and it was they who turned into thieves and ruffians. Even the factories had become chary of giving jobs to the refugees, for they were sure to make trouble. The sorrowful memories of partition had started receding, so it was natural for everybody to feel irritated at having

119

these extra millions foisted upon them. Nobody bothered to remember any more why so many people had become rootless, homeless.

The only reason the political parties took an interest in the refugees was to swell their own ranks with refugee members and workers. Actually they had no interest in their problems. The refugees, too, had been unable to group together on their own. That was the beginning of more misery for them.

The first few days, the head of the Dutta family turned up in person with his henchmen, to talk things over with the senior members of the colony. He could not enter the dance hall, where at one time his family had sat and watched dancing girls display their skills. He had to be content with sitting on the paved altar under the mango tree.

Mr Dutta had politely said that it was wonderful for so many people to have found a haven on his property. He was absolutely gratified. But his circumstances had also been reduced over time. And he too had to live. He could make a reasonable income out of selling the fruit from the garden here. So he proposed that the colony members let him have renewed access to the property.

The settlers had almost agreed to this proposal. For they still felt a remnant of guilt at having occupied another man's land. They did not think it unfair to give the landlord some of his rights back. But the next proposal was more perplexing.

Whenever Mr. Dutta and his companions came and sat under the mango tree for talks, all the members of the colony would stand around in a circle. He always wore loose tops of the finest of superfine cottons, his *dhoti* fell beautifully in folds, he had a silver-mounted walking stick, and his pepper-and-salt-moustache looked very well-nourished under his nose. He would try to pinch the cheeks of the children, but they always ran away. When he sat down, he would take out a packet of expensive foreign cigarettes and distribute them among the senior members of the colony. Haradhan inevitably took two or three at once.

Mr. Dutta's second proposal was this. Let the settlers

all stay here forever, he had absolutely no objection to that (a short speech here, full of sympathy). But the kind of haphazard tenements they had erected for themselves, was not quite acceptable. He was prepared to measure out separate pieces of land for each family according to their needs—but the houses must be built in rows, in a nice, orderly fashion. For those who had to transfer their houses, he was ready to pay compensation. Not only that, he would give them five to seven hundred rupees extra to make up for their trouble. In return, he wanted to lease out the piece of land which would fall vacant next to the pond, to the plywood factory.

'I hope nobody has any objections to this proposal. It will be to everyone's advantage, isn't that so? Afterwards, all of you can live in peace. What do you say?'

The simple, inoffensive colony people had not quite been able to understand this. Startled, they had looked at each other.

What could be the meaning of all this? After untold suffering, they had had a chance to settle down, but what was this move? They were torn between dread and anxiety of the unknown, and the desire to reach out and grab something profitable. Especially the lure of that extra five or seven hundred rupees in a lump sum. They had not seen so much money for ages. It would surely be paid in brand-new notes, rustling together. How beautiful the smell, what comfort to the fingers to touch it!

So they dithered. None of them could give a definite answer, everyone started shouting at the same time. Some of the older men were almost ready to give in for greed of that money. But the young men were against any change in the *status quo*. Arjun was a boy at the time. Nobody paid attention to his judgements. So he did not join the crowd, just wandered about on his own with his dog. And his crazed brother would say to him, 'Don't worry, Arjun. You'll see. Hindustan and Pakistan will become one country again. And we'll take this dog back with us. We won't abandon him.'

The landlord went to and fro like this for a month. His smile grew sweeter by the day, he brought more expensive cigarettes, and even candy for the children.

The people in the colony kept on arguing among themselves and would not give one another a hearing. They had no leader, no adviser. But still, one fact remained: that those who had never been evicted from their own homestead, could never understand what a sorrow it could be. Those who had once had that experience shuddered at the thought of breaking down their homes again. But even they might finally have agreed in the face of temptation. It was only Grandfather Nishi who kept on objecting in his sightless, broken-voiced manner. Even about the first proposal he had said that to allow the Duttas access to the trees meant letting them have the run of the whole orchard again. That would mean that the building of houses in the orchard by other people would remain invalid under law. Would the Duttas give them written, legal documentation for the pieces of land to be allotted? Never. It was much better to keep staying on just as they were. Then, some day, there could be a chance of the government acknowledging their rights. Several other colonies had already received such acknowledgement. If the Duttas wanted compensation for their property, let them go and fight it out with the government.

Perhaps, Grandfather Nishi's arguments would have been ignored by most people. But, suddenly, there was a further complication to the situation. This was when representatives of the Rehabilitation Department came and started sniffing around. They made tempting proposals for resettlement in the Andaman Islands or in Dandakaranya. Every person would have his own homestead, land for cultivation, cash doles and the like. It never occurred to the officials that none of the people in the colony had ever been a peasant. Arjun's brother went up to one government worker and said, 'Listen, why don't you send us back to Faridpur? We'll be better off there. Don't you know, it is all one country again?'

Even though the Rehabilitation Department's proposal was entirely different from that of the Duttas, a certain similarity between the two was noticed by everyone. They realized that there was again an attempt being made to oust them from their homes. That did it! That was enough to re-unite the simple, stubborn people. They did not have sufficient command over the language to deliver polished arguments. So they armed themselves with sticks and drove the government workers off their land. As for the Duttas, they were never allowed to set foot inside the colony again. They threw so many bricks and stones at Mr. Dutta's car, that he was only too happy to escape with his life. He had never been seen in the colony since.

But the Duttas were not going to give up easily. Arjun knew quite well that they were negotiating directly now with the owners of the plywood factory. If the latter could get hold of land for their purposes by their own devices, so much the better. So the proposals were now coming from the factory owners. Kewal Singh had repeatedly said that if at least five families would shift their quarters to the other side of the pond, he would be able to expand his business. And he was prepared to pay a thousand rupees to each family. But Arjun had instructed all of them never to lose possession of their land. Arjun had proved to be a brilliant student, he had a good head on his shoulders, and he knew many people in the city—so a lot of people came to Arjun for advice.

Dibya was speaking to him again.

'You know Arjun, I think you have too much of a prejudice against Kewal Singh. He's not so bad.'

'It's not a question of good and bad, Dibya,' said Arjun. 'It's just that his interests don't coincide with ours. That's all.'

'But Kewal Singh is not a selfish person. Do you think we could have had electricity in here so soon, if he had not allowed us to use his factory connections?'

'We could have done quite well without electricity. If we don't have a place to stay, then lights are not going to do us much good, are they?'

'Yes, but look. During the last riots, the workers from Kewal Singh's factory guarded our colony day and night.'

'Nobody came to attack us during those riots, nor was there a question of an attack. Those factory workers were looking around for a pretext to go and attack the

Muslim villagers near Kaikhali. And you were ready to go along with them! You shouldn't have, Dibya. We have come here to live in peace, not to fight with others.'

This time Dibya's voice sounded very harsh.

'It's all very well for you to say these things,' he said. 'You are quite well off. You people have got the best house to live in, and nobody will try to evict you from there. It's easy to show concern for others from a vantage point like yours.'

'I agree with you there,' said Arjun. 'Sometimes I feel quite ashamed to be living here. But remember, it was the people of our colony who let us stay in this house, Haranda and ourselves, because we were Brahmins.'

'Oh, don't give me all that nonsense about Brahmins. Does that mean you own the world, or what? What do you have left of Brahminhood, anyway?'

'I did say, you know, that we should set up a school here. The children in the colony don't have a chance to go to school and...'

'That's easier said than done. You have become the great scholar now. Why don't you set up the school yourself?'

'How can I, if all of you don't help me? And let me say this, if you all can persuade Haranda to move, then I shall move out immediately. There are only the two of us—my mother and myself—we'll go and stay somewhere else.'

'Yes, I know. You will go off somewhere else, you'll get yourself a fine job—and then you'll forget all these refugees and such-like things.'

Arjun did not bother to reply. A slight smile came to his face. Many people had said this to him already. He himself was not sure how true or false this was. Absently, he started turning over the pages of a book.

Dibya pressed his face against the bars in the window and pleaded with him. 'Listen, Arjun. Can't you find me a job somewhere? I am sick and tired of all this.'

Arjun felt embarrassed.

'A job. What kind of job?'

'Any odd job. You know so many people. Can't you arrange something for me?'

'How can I arrange for a job for you? The market is so bad now.'

'Please do try a little. I am sure you can manage something. I know very well that these days you can get nothing without using your connections. Why don't you talk to some people?'

'Well, you see, the thing is, my friends are not the kind of people who have jobs to give. Besides, I can never ask for any favours from anyone.'

'Not even for me?'

In his embarrassment, Arjun said haltingly, 'Well, all right, I'll see what I can do. But the problem is that my line is so different that...'

Dibya interrupted him vehemently. 'All right, that's enough. You won't have to lift a finger for me. But let me tell you one thing. If you are unable to help anybody in the slightest little way, then you should keep your mouth shut. Why were you lecturing me like that?'

'Dibya, let me explain...'

'I don't have to hear a thing from you. Don't you ever come and say anything to me again. I shall follow my own path.'

'Is this what you had wanted to speak to me about?'

'No, there was something else. But it is no longer necessary to say it.'

Dibya left the window and strode off with long steps. He skirted the pond and went over to the plywood factory. Kewal Singh came out of his room as soon as he saw Dibya coming. Pulling at his beard, with a smirk on his face, Kewal Singh said, 'There you are Dibu*babu*. Why didn't we get to see you last night? I was wondering where you were.'

'I'll come tonight, if I may,' said Dibya gravely. 'Are you having a session tonight?'

'Of course, we are. Why don't you come in for a minute now? There are a couple of things I want to discuss with you.'

Dibya climbed over the broken wall and entered the factory. it had become quite a frequent occurrence in the evenings, to have drinking sessions with locally brewed spirits, within the factory. Dibya too had been invited to join in for the last few days. And, one had to admit, the evening went pleasantly with the help of the best, potent spirits and hot, spiced snacks.

*

Arjun set out from home after a shower and some lunch. It was nice to walk out again after so many days. The world seemed a wonderful place to be in. The dog went skipping along at his side. It would always accompany Arjun up to the main road. It had rained last night. The leaves on the trees looked freshly washed, green. There were new leaves on the mango tree, the ones at the very top copper-coloured, the ones below gleaming green. A *kubo* bird sat somewhere inside the foliage and emitted its characteristic notes. Arjun had never been able to set eyes on the bird.

One of the boys belonging to the families living beside the boundary wall, Kartik, started walking with Arjun. Kartik was full of new complaints about Kewal Singh. But Arjun was tired of listening to all this. He was still unsteady on his feet, like a toddler, his head weighed heavily on his shoulders—it was as if he had to learn to walk anew on the surface of the earth. He wanted to be left alone to enjoy the pleasure.

So he tried to discourage Kartik.

'Why do you have to pay attention to Kewal Singh?' he said. 'What can he do to us? There's still some law in the country.'

'How can we ignore him when his men keep coming into our yards every day? And the smell of that rotting wood!'

'Throw out those men. If you can't do it alone, get together with the others.'

'Listen Arjun, I think it was Kewal Singh who hired ruffians to beat you up.'

'What rot! What does he have to gain by doing that? I don't live near his factory.'

'No, but you do know so many influential people. You are quite capable of calling in the police. If you had not stood firm in your opposition, that fellow would have evicted us ages ago.'

'Don't talk such rubbish, Kartik. People don't beat each other up on such trifling grounds. Probably it is someone who has a deep grudge against me, someone I know nothing about. Go on now, go back home. I have to go to college.'

After Kartik went away, Arjun saw two separate quarrels within the colony. Uncle Haripada's family were carrying on a feud with their neighbours, the language so obscene that you could not bear to listen to it. Yet the children were playing right in front of the houses, and memorizing every single word of abuse. Their parents were using them, so why should they not learn too?

A few steps further on, under the lychee tree, three grown-up boys were fighting about something at the top of their voices. They could not care who else heard them. It was about equal shares in something or other. Their abuse was even stronger than that of their parents, and it looked as if they would start hitting each other any minute. The only person who could stop them now would be Dibya.

Arjun sighed. He had noticed that quarrels and disagreements were much more frequent now within the colony. Had not these people quarrelled in their village? Of course they had. But this was where they really needed to be united. Suppose the Duttas came in again with more honeyed words. Would everybody be able to make a unified stand and throw them out again? The elders who still had memories of days past, were either plunged in gloom, or reduced to painful sighs of nostalgia. And those who had been children when they had come here, those who did not remember the past, or those who had been born here—for them there was no reason to take heed of the past. They were growing up, they wanted jobs, comfort and equality with others. Those things being denied them, all they seemed to do was immerse themselves in the filth of the lower levels of society. At the slightest provocation, they were ready to bare fangs and claws.

Arjun went on. There was Grandfather Nishi in front

of Labonya's house. He was leaning on Naru, trying to listen to the distant sounds of altercation, and kept asking, 'Naru, who are those people, shouting like that? What's going on? Are they having a fight?' Naru could not be bothered to answer. He was concentrating on chewing a guava. Grandfather could see nothing. But he had to know everything. His old, battered heart was still concerned with the well-being of others.

A little farther off, Labonya stood talking to Purnima. Arjun thought for an instant that he would call Labonya and ask why she had never come back to him for help with her studies. But he decided not to. He was in a hurry. His eyes met Labonya's. But she did not say anything either.

Sukhen happened to walk by at this point. He glanced at Labonya's face and then at Arjun. Then he took a few steps forward and burst into a raucous song about a Brahmin's son and a washerman's daughter.

Arjun had not been listening too carefully to the words of the song. But the sly look on Sukhen's face reminded him of what Labonya had told him about Sukhen. Sukhen was still smarting under the disappointment of not being able to marry Labonya. Could it be that he was referring to Arjun as the Brahmin's son? Arjun knew that some people were catty enough to call Labonya a washerman's daughter, simply because her father had a laundry. Good God, is that what they thought of Labonya and himself? He had never had much time to think about such things. Labonya only came to him for a little help with her work. And this was what they all thought of it? The girl really wanted to pass in her examinations, she had such aspirations for a different life—poor girl.

'Sukhen,' called out Arjun. 'Come here for a minute.'

But Sukhen did not linger. He disappeared fast. Arjun debated, for a moment, whether or not to go and grab him. But then he smiled to himself. What was the point of descending into recriminations like everybody else? He stepped outside the colony, slapped the dog on the head saying, 'Go home, Becharam, go home to mother,' and then went on to the bus stop. His thoughts turned from Labonya to Purnima and he could not help sighing. Arjun had once encountered Purnima near the Victoria Memorial.

*

Purnima was speaking to Labonya.

'Why didn't you go Labi?'

'Where to?'

'You said you were going to find out which college you had been assigned to take the final examinations.'

'Oh that. Yes. I'll go in a while.'

'Why didn't you go along with Arjun*da*? He went by just now.'

'Why should I? He was not going in my direction.'

Purnima pressed her lips into a sly smile.

'Yes, but just think, you could have travelled together up to Shyambazar at least. He would have paid your bus fare.'

Labonya looked sharply at Purnima. She had understood the implication behind the words perfectly. But since it was nothing obvious, she could not answer back. Purnima, however, quickly changed her tone.

'If you ever meet Arjun*da*, she said innocently, 'he's sure to pay your bus fare. He did it once for me. Tell me when you want to go today. I have to go to the office too. We can leave together.'

'I'll go around twelve-thirty or one.'

'Fine. That's when I'll go too.'

'You mean to say you can go to work any time you please? You seem to go out at different times on different days.'

Purnima made a face.

'Oh yes, it doesn't matter as long as you turn up. There isn't that much to do. It certainly is more pleasure than work.'

Purnima was the only girl in the colony who always went around in sandals. She was quite given to little luxuries. A touch of black around her eyes, cheap silk saris on her body. Her complexion was very light, but her cheeks had already caved in, the collar bones very prominent.

Purnima spoke again, in softened tones.

'Your exams start the day after tomorrow, don't they? Why don't you borrow my *kotki* sari to wear? You have always liked that one.'

Labonya's eyes gleamed. Normally she just wanted to avoid having anything to do with Purnima. But the offer of the sari was too tempting to refuse. Never in her life had Labonya worn an expensive sari. And Purnima had so many of them. Labonya did not even have a respectable sari to wear for her examinations. She had decided on wearing her mother's ancient *jamdani* sari. It was coming apart in places, but she could hide that.

'Do you have it laundered,' Labonya asked eagerly. 'Otherwise I can wash it myself.'

'Oh no, you don't have to do a thing. It's washed, pressed and ready to wear. I haven't worn it in ages. You'll look lovely in it. But tell me one thing, Labi. We eat the same food, our rice comes from the same ration shop. So how come only you are blooming with health more and more every day?'

Purnima's eyes shamelessly raked Labonya's full breasts, rounded arms and slim waist. Labonya's whole face became suffused with colour. In low tones, she said, 'You are all right yourself. You are five or six years older than I am. But nobody can guess that.'

Purnima slapped her hips.

'Nonsense, my dear. How many people turn around to look at me? Listen, Labi. Will you come with me to my office one day, once your exams are over?'

'What will I do there?'

'You can meet all my friends. I have spoken about you to many of them. If you want, you can even get a job there.'

'If I pass this time, I intend to get a job in the mornings at some school. In the afternoons, I shall attend the university.'

'What, more studies? Listen, if you do too much of that, you will become a stick of dry wood. You'll see. Besides, what good is a teaching job these days?'

'My father says he won't let me work anywhere else.'

'But you get paid so little there. All you do is shout at

those kids until you drop dead. And look at my office. So many advantages. You can go any time you want, and you just have to dress well. No other problems. With your looks, my dear, you will be hired on the spot.'

A sharp rejoinder escaped Labonya.

'Is that what they do in your office—hire people for their looks? What kind of an office is it?'

Purnima gave her a broad grin.

'Come off it, Labonya. I've seen it all. The only thing of value women have is their looks. If you are really ugly, then you can be loaded with talent, but nobody will spare a moment for you. You are still young and healthy. Enjoy all the pleasures you can. Otherwise you'll just have to rot by yourself.'

The colour drained out of Labonya's face. Such obvious and open hints about her body insulted her deeply. But she was going to have her say too. Anger reddening her face, she burst out, 'Aren't you ashamed of yourself, Purnimadi? Do you think I really don't know what kind of office you have? You go to Dharmatala and spend your afternoons sitting in tea shops. And unknown men come...'

Purnima pounced on her at once.

'What! What did you say?'

'Yes, I did say it. You come from such a well-respected family and yet you can...'

'You lying little bitch. A thousand curses on your head for lying like this. I go and sit in tea shops, do I? Well, all right, so I do. So what? What has it got to do with anybody? Do I have to listen to comments on my movements from a washerwoman?'

"Yes, it is better to be a washerwoman, even a serving woman than to be like you."

'That's all you are good for anyway. I can see your future quite well. All this pride because you have been going to college. What about your morals, then? Messing around shamelessly with Arjun. At every opportunity you slip into his room and like a real whore you...'

'Careful now, Purnimadi, Don't you dare say anything like that again."

"Why shouldn't I? What can you do to stop me? I'll say

131

just what I please, and to everybody too. When Arjun gives you a swollen belly...'

Red hot fury blazed in Labonya's face, but the tears also rushed to her eyes. In moments of anger, Labonya lost all sense of place and person. She was almost on the verge of springing on Purnima and scratching and biting her. But she managed to control herself with a desperate effort. She spat fiercely on the ground.

"That's what I think of you. I'd rather hang myself than borrow your sari."

"Listen, you won't even find a rope to hang yourself with."

Labonya saw her father returning home, and quickly went inside. But Purnima kept standing there and screaming abuses for a while, linking Labonya's name with Arjun's. Not that Biswanath paid the slightest attention to that. He had trained himself never to listen to other people.

Purnima decided to go to the pond and have a bath to cool off. By an unwritten rule, one side of the pond was reserved for women, the other for men. There was no one on the women's side, but the men's side was quite crowded. Purnima stood on the steps in front of them, removed her clothes and rubbed oil all over herself. Then she soaped her bare body for a long time. Let those greedy fools stare their fill at her. When she was really angry, Purnima enjoyed the sensation of considering the entire race of men as beggars. At this moment she was giving them alms, the freedom to look at her body.

After lunch, she decided to put on the very same *kotki* sari, she had offered Labonya. Then she chewed a *paan* to make her mouth red, took a red bag and started walking—her hips swinging more than usual. This was how Purnima went to office. She looked proudly at Labonya's house. Let that bitch see her, Purnima just didn't give a damn.

Purnima's father, Haradhan, was still hanging around Biswanath's shop. The owner was not around, there was only little Naru minding the shop. Haradhan had been trying to wheedle some money out of the boy. The sight of his daughter brought him quickly to the street.

He walked with her for a while before saying in low tones, 'Puni, can't you give me just five rupees? I have been asking you for days.'

'I did give it to you, a couple of days back.'

'That's a lie. You gave me some last Saturday.'

'Well, what do you want with money now?'

'Please, my dear, do let me have it. It's your own father. It will bring you good luck to give something to your old father.'

'I'll give it to you when I get back from the office. I don't have any money now.'

'What shall I do with it so late at night? Just look into your purse, my dear. I am sure you'll find some. I don't even have enough to buy some cigarettes.'

The bus was coming. Purnima could not delay any longer. She opened her bag with irritation and took out two rupees, saying, 'Here you are. But let me tell you, if you keep on pestering me like this every day, I won't come back home.'

'Don't be so angry, child. There's nothing to be angry about.'

VII

'Come and sit down Arjun,' said Maya. 'Abanish*da* is in the bathroom.'

Arjun smiled.

'How long has he been there?'

Maya smiled too. Once Abanish went into the bathroom, he would not be out for an hour. First, he would take something along to read. Besides, just having a bath was a long, leisurely affair with him. Strangely enough, no sound ever came out of the bathroom—you would hardly think there was anybody there. Even if the house caught fire, it is doubtful whether Abanish would come out in less than his allotted time.

Maya sat and talked with Arjun for a while and then went in, saying, 'I'll be back soon.' Obviously, she was very busy with something, but she could not leave Arjun sitting there all by himself. Maya was a very polite person.

'Why don't you go in,' said Arjun, 'and finish what you were doing. I shall be quite happy to sit here and read.'

'No, no, no. I am not really busy at all. I'll be back in a second.'

And Maya was adamant. She really had no pressing business, she said. Finally, Arjun just got up.

'Why don't I just go upstairs and talk to Shukla for a bit? Is she at home?'

'I don't really know Arjun,' said Maya with a smile.

That is, it was impossible for anyone in the house to keep tabs on Shukla's movements, her comings and goings. She was here one minute and there the next. She must have had wheels under her feet, that girl. It was

134

just not possible for her to be in one place for long.

Shukla's room was on the second floor. On the first floor, there was a long balcony with big slabs of coloured tiles. As he walked, Arjun started placing his footsteps in the centre of each slab, just like a child. The stairs were right at the end of the balcony.

A sudden sound of heavily squeaking shoes made him look up. Abanish's father. A huge man with a handsome, dignified presence. He had a man on either side of him, one carrying his medical bag, the other muttering something, probably the case history of some patient being crammed into his mind within this space of time. Shukla's father never had a moment to spare. He was perpetually listening to descriptions of other people's illnesses.

As soon as his eyes met Arjun's, he nodded and said, 'Hello, hope everything is fine with you.'

Arjun nodded back. But by that time Dr. Mukherjee had gone past him. He was an extremely absent-minded man. How he could manage to remember the names of a thousands of drugs was a great mystery. It was obvious that he had not recognized Arjun. Yet, it had been he who had made all the arrangements for Arjun to be treated in hospital. He could not have remembered that, otherwise he would have made some enquiries about Arjun's health. To him, Arjun was just someone he had encountered in his own house, whom he had to greet with a few words. It was Arjun's opinion that if Shukla's father happened to come face to face with a burglar who was making off with a lot of things, even then he would ask him how he was, and walk on.

Shukla's younger sister, Tandra, had her room near the first floor staircase. This was the one person in this family who was a shy loner. Arjun had never seen a crowd of friends in her room. Tandra was quite wrapped up in her studies.

Arjun saw her in her room and asked, 'Is your sister upstairs?'

'Probably. I saw her just a while back.'

'Don't you have classes today?'

'No, the students have called a strike.'

'We used to go to college even on the days we had a strike. That was the time to go and have a nice chat with your friends.'

Tandra just gave him a shy smile in answer. The same house, the same atmosphere, the same liberties, and yet the children had turned out to be so different from each other.

There was a telephone on every floor in the house. Shukla was talking on the phone upstairs on the balcony. She still wore a housecoat over her night-gown. She had probably been in bed all this time, there was nothing unusual about that. Arjun stopped short as he came to the end of the stairs. Was he supposed to go up or not? One thing was certain. Whoever else may have been embarrassed at being caught by an outsider in this garb, it would not be Shukla. Her expression did not change at all. She put her hand over the mouthpiece and said, 'Go and sit in my room. I'll be along in a minute.'

Not that time signified anything. Shukla on the phone was like Abanish in the bath. Once she got started, she could go on for hours. God alone knew what she had to talk about! Arjun had never telephoned Shukla.

A long balcony, with black and white tiles on the floor. Spotlessly clean. Potted flowering plants arranged next to the rails. To visit a house like this should have made Arjun uncomfortable, but, somehow, it did not. Awkwardness did not exist here. The children of this family—each inhabited their own rooms, and nobody was much concerned with the affairs of others.

There was no common living room in the house. Both the sitting rooms on the ground floor were used as waiting rooms for the patients. Shukla's father had three other doctors assisting him in the rooms downstairs. So each member of the family had a portion of his own room done up as a sitting room. And there were seating arrangements on the balconies as well.

Shukla's room was a huge one. A bed on one side, with a soft mattress and snowy white sheets. On the other side were two couches, several chairs and cane stools, a record player and the dart board on the wall. There was a smaller room leading off this one, which was like a wardrobe. Shukla kept her clothes there and got dressed there as well. The room next to hers belonged to the brother next to Abanish. Since he was in England now, with his wife, his room was kept locked up.

Shukla was a most untidy person. The whole room was strewn with her belongings. Books, lipsticks, loose change. This kind of indifference could only come from having everything in abundance.

Arjun suddenly thought of Labonya. Labonya had been mildly envious of Shukla. And why not? Shukla's whole life was so remote from Labonya's. But, really, you could not envy Shukla—whimsical, so restless, with such excessive vitality, all together so extraordinarily beautiful. True, she was remote from the lives of people like Labonya. But one enjoyed the very sight of her so much. Can one see the Taj Mahal and think enviously, 'Why is my bedroom not like that?'

Shukla never would accept failure. Whatever Labonya could do, Shukla managed just as well. For instance, there were numerous servants in Shukla's household. None of the family ever had to do anything for themselves. But if you asked Shukla to wipe the floors, she would immediately tighten her sari, and set to work. The whole house would be wiped clean, and impeccably too. Just as she had sat down and washed the dishes after that picnic in Naihati. She took life as an adventure; so she could face everything with glad spirits.

There was only one thing that Shukla had not learnt to do yet—to swim. She had almost drowned on the day of the picnic. Yet she loved the water. Most women do. Deep, secret thoughts surface in their minds whenever they sit next to any water. But the best way to love water is by learning to swim; it is like loving with your body.

Shukla had been bathing in the pond in the country estate at Naihati with three or four other girls, when she had happened to drift into deep water. None of the girls had known how to swim either—as is usual with most Calcutta girls. Arjun had heard them screaming at the top of their voices. And even that had been fortuitous. He had given chase to a runaway chicken and had come near the pond. So the race to rob one living being of its life, had ended up saving another's. He had jumped straight into the water, there had been no time to throw his clothes off.

Shukla certainly was a strange creature. How she had lost her temper with Arjun after having been saved from drowning! As soon as she had come to, she had broken out in pungent tones. 'Who asked you to pull me out? I was going to find out what death by drowning was like.'

Arjun had laughed.

'That would not have been possible, Shukla. You can't know or find anything once you are dead.'

'Well, I could have, up to the moment of death, couldn't I? I was losing my senses, gasping and choking—it was quite a novel experience for me.'

'You are trying to be clever, aren't you? That may have been very unusual, but once you were dead you couldn't have come back to life. So how would you have talked about your new sensations?'

Abanishda had intervened at that point.

'Go on Arjun, throw her into the water again since she is so eager to die.'

But still Shukla had gone on at Arjun.

'Why did you have to save my life? Who asked you to?'

'No one. It's just a human instinct. Do you remember, I hit you hard in the water? That was also instinct. For I was trying to save myself. You had wrapped yourself round me in such a fashion that I would have drowned myself, if I hadn't hit you.'

This reference to having wrapped herself round Arjun, in front of her friends, had not pleased Shukla at all. She had looked very annoyed. Probal had started expressing his regrets, 'I have a life-saving certificate, and I never heard a thing. Wasted a chance to do my thing.'

Some time later Shukla had spoken to Arjun privately.

'I don't like being beholden to anybody. It's fine for you to save my life. But how am I to pay you back?'

Again Arjun had had to smile at her absurdity.

'Your grandmother is still alive,' he had told her. 'Go and ask her if she has one of those cowries with holes in them. Old ladies often have such things. If you do get one, give it to me, and we'll be quits. A man's life is not worth more than that.'

'What! Are you trying to tell me my life is worth only that trivial amount?'

'Why should your life be any more precious than that of others? They are all worth the same.'

It had been afternoon, on the edge of that very pond. Arjun's words had made Shukla look thoughtful.

'Thank God, you've said that,' she had said. 'Otherwise, if you had taken this opportunity to start talking about love and that sort of nonsense, I would have slapped you on the face.'

Arjun had been amazed. How did love come into the matter at all? If in his place there had been a woodsman or a fisherman, he too would have jumped into the water to save Shukla. Would that person then have said, 'I did this for love of you.'

'Are you afraid to hear people talk about love?' he had asked.

'Afraid? No, certainly not. In fact, I've just been hearing about it from another person. It's only that I can't bear to have two people talking about it on the same day.'

*

Arjun glanced out of the room. Shukla was still on the phone. He found he could not sit still. He wandered restlessly all over the room. Turned over the pages of books. How did Shukla find time to read so much? He suddenly heard a humming noise. Where was that coming from? Oh yes, just look at that mad girl, she had forgotten to switch off the record player. Perhaps it had been left like that all night.

The feathered darts were lying on the low table. Arjun started fiddling with them. Shukla's friends loved to play with them. So did Shukla. There was nobody in the room now. Perhaps he could try a few shots...

Arjun picked up three of the darts. With a bit of concentration, he aimed one at the centre of the board on the wall. But it went quite off the mark, and hit the fourth circle. So, this was a rather difficult game. Not as easy as he had thought. Actually, it was quite difficult to balance a feathered arrow in one's hand. But to land so far off! At one time Arjun had been quite a good marksman. He used to practise throwing stones at mango and guava trees. In fact, at one stage, he had been good enough to pick a mango off the topmost branch. He had also acquired a catapult and had carried it around everywhere. But when he had killed the stork with it, his brother had been extremely unhappy, and ever since, the catapult had been left untouched.

Arjun took a few steps backwards. He closed one eye and stared at the centre point. He shut off all the corners of his mind and brought it to bear on that one point. This time he had to hit the bull's-eye. His body became absolutely motionless. He threw the dart.

He had not really expected the dart to hit the centre. But not a hair's breadth off, there was the dart, piercing the centre point. The first one going so awry, and this one hitting the mark—both were equally surprising. But there was nobody to watch Arjun's failure or success. This was an empty room. He decided not to throw the third dart. Who knows where this one would land?

'Who planted the dart in the middle? You?'

'Yes.'

'Liar. Tell me the truth now. How close were you? Did you stand ten yards away from the board?'

Arjun laughed.

'Are you crazy? I just wanted to startle you. So I walked up to the board and pushed the dart in.'

'Yes, I could have guessed that anyway. It's not so easy to hit the centre. So far, nobody has been able to do it. You least of all.'

'Why? Why not me?'

'Well, find out. Try if you can do it.'

'You think I can't? It's not just that point on the board either. You see the picture of the bird on your calendar? Well, I can hit the bird in the eye from here. There was a time when I killed many birds with my catapult.'

The calendar hung on the opposite wall. A foreign airline was advertised on it. Instead of a plane, there was a flying hawk, holding exactly the same pose.

Shukla patted her hair into place as she said, 'Stop bragging so much. Show me what you can do. Catapults and darts are not the same thing.'

Arjun started taking aim.

'All right,' he said, 'I shall hit the bird. But how much will you bet on it?'

'Why should I bet on it? Can't you do anything without a wager?'

'No, it's hard to find enthusiasm unless there is a bet on.'

'Hit first, then we'll talk about betting.'

Arjun leant his head back a little, closed one eye and again concentrated on his aim with all his mind. Shukla looked like she had not yet washed her face after getting up. There was a film of sleep over her face. Though it was so late, she had not even run a comb through her hair. She looked as though she was savouring some kind of a languid pleasure. She looked at Arjun and a light smile spread over her face. Still smiling, she said, 'I had no idea it took so long to take aim. You will even surpass chess players.'

'Stop chattering.'

'Oh do, please, tell me what you are seeing at this moment. Then I'll know if you have a chance.'

'Nothing but the bird's eye.'

Shukla's laughter rang out merrily. Without turning his head, Arjun reproved her.

'Don't laugh. I can't concentrate.'

'I'm sorry. It's just that I remembered something then.'

'What?'

'It's no use telling you. You study science. You people don't read anything else and you won't understand it anyway.'

She started laughing quietly again. Arjun straightened up and turned towards her with a smile, saying, 'No, I won't try this one now.'

'Be honest and admit that you can't.'

Arjun threw the dart towards the ceiling and caught it in his hands again.

141

'This sort of thing is all right in childhood,' he said. 'As a kid I would have been terribly excited by this challenge. Now I feel like laughing. If I can't make it, then it doesn't matter. But if I do hit the mark, then I might feel a bit conceited. That's not worth it.'

'I know what you are trying to do, you evasive character. Here, let me have the dart.'

Shukla did not take much aim, she just threw the dart from where she was sitting. It did not quite hit the bird's eye, but it did hit the calendar page, close to it, and then fell to the floor.

'You see,' said Shukla in triumph.

Arjun clapped his hands.

'Great! You could easily have been a female Robin Hood. But see, just because you nearly succeeded, there's a conceited, self-satisfied expression on your face.'

'You can come here and practise now and then. Then you will be able to do it too.'

'No, thank you. Your room is full of people most of the time. This is the first time I've seen it empty. Besides, it is time for you to change. I might as well be off.'

'Why, does it bother you to see me like this?'

In point of fact, uneasiness or embarrassment was not the issue at all. There were deerskin slippers on Shukla's feet, her legs were bare to the knee, as she leant back on the couch. Through the housecoat, you could catch a glimpse of her flimsy nightgown, and beyond that, of the smooth skin of her body. This dishevelled apparel, this stance of sitting carelessly—all this had an unbearable quality of beauty. No, it did not make him uneasy, it only made him aware of a deep sadness.

'No,' said Arjun, 'But that doesn't mean you have to loll around like this all day.'

Shukla stretched lazily.

'I don't feel like doing anything today. But I know I have to get ready soon. Why are you here at this time of day? Don't have any new prospects of hooliganism to pursue?'

'Me? Hooliganism?'

'Yes, what other kind of person would go around

breaking his head and being beaten up?'

'The fact is, I came at this time today, because I knew for sure that you would be alone. So, I just wanted to talk to you.'

'Don't you expect me to believe that. My brother must have disappeared into the bathroom.'

'No, no, I really didn't come to see Abanishda. I only wanted to see you today.'

'Stop it, will you. You've never come here only to see me. I know my brother has taken two weeks' leave from university. That's why you have come to the house, to discuss your precious work with him. Then, when you saw my brother was in the bathroom, you came up to my room to pass the time.'

'How on earth do you manage to find out when your brother is on leave, and when he is not?' he asked. 'When do you get to see him anyway?'

'At mealtimes, of course. I meet the whole family there twice a day.'

'Is that the only time you people meet each other?'

'Yes, it is a bit like that. While we are in Calcutta, we follow the rule of sitting down to our meals at the same time, together. My father is also present there. It's hard to get to see him otherwise. Oh, that reminds me. I must go and tell the cook I won't be in for lunch today.'

'Why? Where are you off to?'

'We are eating out.'

'Then you'll have to get dressed and leave soon, won't you? I had thought that since I'd found you all alone, I wouldn't do any work today. Just sit and talk.'

'Why don't you come with us too? Yes, do please come. We plan to go to Diamond Harbour.'

'We? Who else is going?'

'Probal, Akhtar, Ranajoy and Barun. They are all supposed to come here at twelve. And on the way we shall pick up Jayanti, Nandita and Mandira. We have two cars going. Do come, it will be such fun.'

'Yes, your usual crowd. No, I don't think I'll come.'

'Why not? Don't you like them?'

'Why shouldn't I like them? But what I really wanted to do was talk to you alone.'

'Listen, come along with us. Mandira will be there. She's quite soft on you.'

'But I just want to talk to you alone.'

Shukla got up, wandered around the room, and found a silver-mounted comb. She plunged it into her hair and said lightly, 'Very well. We still have half an hour. Tell me whatever you have to say.'

Arjun had to smile again.

'You really are a funny girl. How can I say something within an allotted time. All I was trying to say was that I wanted to have a long, leisurely chat with you, and only you. How can I do that in half an hour?'

'Yes, I know, that's what you've been saying all along. But you haven't really started to talk, have you?'

'Tell me, who were you talking to on the phone for such a long time?'

'Naughty, naughty! Why this curiosity? Don't you know, you are never supposed to ask a girl about these things? Of course you don't, you East Bengali rustic.'

'No, I don't. You are quite right, there are lots of things I don't know. I am sure none of my forefathers ever dreamed that I would sit here in a room alone with a girl like you, wearing only her housecoat.'

Shukla did not quite catch his meaning. However, the reference to the housecoat made her look at herself as if she realized for the first time that it was not quite proper to see anybody in this state of undress. But she did not get flustered either. She threw the comb on the bed and said, 'Yes, I suppose I should really get out of these things. They'll all be here soon. Wait for me, I'll just take a quick shower.'

Shukla probably would not take as long as as Abanish in the shower. But still Arjun tried to leave.

'No, you'd better get ready in peace,' he said. 'You'll have to leave soon. I'll go downstairs.'

But Shukla turned on him with a frown and spoke in an almost aggressive manner.

'Sit down. All you can think of saying is you have to leave.'

There it was, the same stance of pride. Some girls know quite well, that they look attractive in a temper,

144

aggressiveness suits them. That was why Shukla spoke like she did. But there are some others, who do not understand it. Even if it does not become them, they keep having tantrums. They are definitely to be pitied.

Nevertheless, Arjun got up, just to annoy Shukla.

'No, I have to go now.'

Like a swooping bird, Shukla was close to him in an instant. She placed a hand on his shoulder and pressed it firmly.

'You listen to what I say. Sit down this minute.'

But as soon as Arjun raised his hand to take hold of hers, she twirled around like a dancer, released herself and moved away. From the other side of the door she said, 'Just give me five minutes. No more...'

The sudden movement brought the fragrance of her hair to Arjun in a wave. It was not any kind of perfumed oil, just her own smell. For whatever reason, he had never seen Shukla's hair in a braid. Nor did she ever put it up in a chignon. Shukla liked to wear hair long and unbound, falling in a cloud down her back.

Shukla herself was also a student with the science faculty. But she was an avid reader of all sorts of books. In her room were scattered journals like The *National Geographic*, books of English and Bengali poetry, the works of Tagore, several novels by Bibhutibhusan and Manik Bandopadhyay. She took no care of her books— she left them lying around. Sometimes, one could find Shukla dancing at the fancy-dress parties at the YWCA. But she was totally different from all the other girls who went dancing there. None of them could rattle off Tagore's poetry from memory. How on earth did she find time to do all this?

Arjun picked up another feathered dart, and threw it at the bird in the calendar without taking much aim. It hit the bird in the eye. This was amazing. Had he suddenly acquired magical abilities today? But he would not play this game in front of Shukla. It was a minor thing. Not worth showing off.

They came up the stairs with resounding footsteps, four well-formed, handsome young men, their eyes bright with laughter. Barun, Probal, Akhtar and Ranajoy. They were almost like Shukla's bodyguards.

'Hello Arjun,' said Barun. 'Been here long? Where's Shukla?'

'I hope you are coming with us today Arjun,' said Akhtar. 'Sorry I could not come and visit you in the hospital. I had to go to North Bengal then.'

'Of course, he'll come,' said Ranajoy. 'All these days you have been laid up in bed. Come along with us today and you'll have a good time.'

Probal was sparing with his words. He smiled a little, inclined his head towards Arjun and asked, 'Have you recovered completely?'

They lit cigarettes without hesitation, pulled chairs out noisily, sat down, and started playing loud Western music on the record player. The whole atmosphere of the room changed. Arjun had not smoked a single cigarette in all this time. Now he lit one offered by one of them. Ranajoy and Akhtar never smoked anything but foreign cigarettes. They stubbed them out in the ashtray before they were half finished. Arjun had decided that if he ever happened to make any money, he too would blow some with abandon. He too wanted to enjoy the sensation of finding out the meaninglessness of money. It was more necessary for him than for many others, because he had gone down to the railway tracks in the middle of the night, like a covetous animal, to search out the coin which he himself had thrown away.

Arjun started thinking how much of a misfit he was in this situation. In looks and in health, perhaps, he was just the same as the others. But there was a deeper difference. Perhaps he had managed to get the top position in one subject in his MSc exams but that credential carried no particular weight with these people. None of them were particularly poor students, except perhaps Ranajoy. And Ranajoy was a fantastic tennis player. He had even gone to Japan for some kind of championship. But what mattered was that none of them lived in a slum-like habitation as Arjun did. They came from families worth boasting about. And that was what really counted. Arjun threw away his cigarette and got up to leave.

At that moment Shukla came back into the room. She

was wearing a magnificent sari with slanting stripes in black and yellow—at first glance, she resembled a leopardess.

'There you are,' said Ranajoy. 'Ready, I hope. We must not be late.'

'Shukla, why doesn't Arjun want to come with us?' asked Barun. 'Why don't you try and persuade him?'

That was exactly what Shukla had been doing a little while ago. But by now she had changed her mind. Her smile had a hint of cruelty in it as she said, 'Why should he come along? He will now go downstairs to sit with my brother and pore over his books. That's about all he is good for. As if academic work is going to get him everything he wants. We can't do anything with these good-boy types. Leave him alone. Let's go.'

Arjun too smiled at her. The look of pride was back on Shukla's face.

VIII

Dibya and three other young men were taken on at the plywood factory. Even Sukhen quit the bakery and joined them. That was when Kewal Singh's depredations became substantial.

He was absolutely determined to acquire an extra piece of land, to expand his factory. The other side of the factory was completely built up and there was not the ghost of a chance of getting land there. So the easiest option for Kewal Singh was to wrest land away from the colony. He had also managed to come to some secret agreement with the Duttas. They were a comparatively impoverished family now, so they were desperate to get something out of their huge estate. After all, the maximum amount of compensation you could get from the government was five to seven thousand rupees per *bigha*. But on the open market, even a twentieth of that much land, was valued at four-and-a-half-thousand.

The workers from the factory were no longer content with just entering the colony at all odd hours of the day and night. They even stood guard over the sheets of drying wood. At night they would come in noisily and wander about, sometimes tapping on doors and windows, sometimes making fearful drunken noises. It was undeniably oppression. But who was to protest? Some of the boys in the colony had also decided to join them. The former spirit of unity no longer existed within the colony. Each person was busy pursuing his own interests. Many of the families were like rootless trees, whose topmost branches have started to wither. Kewal Singh was a shrewd man. He was doing his utmost to foment division and disaffection between the people of the colony.

Somebody had to redress this. A lot of people still held Grandfather Nishi in respect. So a small meeting was held in the courtyard of Biswanath's house. The elderly members were present and even Dibya's group could be seen in one corner. Not that anybody had yet been able to give any definite opinions. They were all arguing in loud voices.

Grandfather called out, 'Labi, Labi, my dear. Do go and fetch Arjun.'

Dibya protested at once.

'Why do we need to call Arjun? He doesn't have anything new to say.'

'No, Dibya, it's better to have him here. After all he is an educated boy.'

'Fat lot of good his education has done him. Do you think he has the answers to everything? He doesn't have any problems. He lives in a proper house.'

This reference to the house made Haran fidget with unease. He sat down on the floor of the porch and said, 'Let him come. Let us hear what he has to say. He may have links with the big chiefs in the police force.'

'Huh! As if there aren't any other educated men in Calcutta.'

Labonya came out of the house at this point.

'What do you want?' she demanded.

'Go on, child,' said Grandfather Nishi. 'Go and bring Arjun over here.'

'I'm busy, I can't go now. Send Naru.'

'No, no, Labi,' said Sukhen in dulcet tones. 'You are the one who must go. Naru won't be able to explain everything properly. You can persuade Arjun to come, even if he says he is busy. Tell him this is an urgent matter.'

Labonya directed a furious glance at Sukhen.

'Why don't you go yourself, then?' she asked.

Labonya had stopped going to Arjun's house as much as she used to, after the ugly implications flung at her the other day by Purnima. Biswanath stepped in to help her.

'That's all right, Labi. You go inside and study. I'll go

149

and get Arjun myself.'

Labonya was still standing there when Arjun turned up.

'So Labi,' he said. 'How are the exams going? How many have you had so far?'

'Three. I suppose I am doing all right.'

'You said you'd come for some help with your work. Why didn't you?'

'It wasn't necessary.'

'Well, what are you standing here for, wasting your time. Go inside and work. You must do well this time.'

'Come Arjun,' said Grandfather Nishi, 'come and sit down. You must have heard everything. This sort of thing can't be allowed to go on. But what do you think we can do?'

Arjun did not sit down. But he spoke modestly.

'What can I say? You all will know best what needs to be done.'

'Let's call in the police', suggested Haran. 'Those Punjabis won't cool down until you let the police loose on them.'

Haran, as a taxi driver, had an obsession about his rivals in the business, most of whom were Punjabis. And the only class of people he himself held in fear were the police.

Suddenly Dhiren Shikdar started shouting.

'And what about my boy? Those people are always beating him up. Why does nobody take notice of that? I don't have ten children—just this one precious child. We escaped with our lives from the hands of the Muslims. Was it only to be beaten up by these non-Bengalis? What do you say? Eh, what do you all have to say?'

That did it. They all started clamouring at once. Most of them had their grievances, but they were not going to give the others a hearing. Arjun leant against the grapefruit tree and stared at the ground. All these people had been close to him, yet he had moved so far away from them. To hear them vociferating in their unrefined language, using foolish arguments, made him want to laugh, only to strike him with sadness again. Even when they were shouting out phrases like, 'my house', there was no strength of conviction in their voices, for the land still did not belong to them. Even now, they were known as refugees, people without a home.

Grandfather Nishi was trying to say something but his voice was drowned in the ongoing clamour. Finally Dibya got up, and his words boomed out over everything else.

'Quiet, everybody. It's no use all of us speaking together. One by one, please. Grandfather here is presiding over the meeting. Let us listen to him first.'

The noise started subsiding and Grandfather's voice could be heard again.

'Yes, Dibya. You see how things are. You explain to them'

'What is there for me to say?' asked Dibya. 'You know it all. In my opinion we should at least consider Kewal Singh's proposition. If you have to co-exist with the man, you can't fight him all the time. Besides, he hasn't said anything unfair. If five of the families have to transfer their accommodation from one side of the pond to the other, it's not going to be the end of the world for them, is it? After all, he has promised to pay for the rebuilding of the houses.'

Arjun raised his head.

'No, Dibya,' he said, 'that's just not on.'

'Why not?'

'You don't understand...'

'Oh, so I don't understand and you understand everything?'

'That's not the point. Just listen to me. Whoever has possession has a lot of right to the land. Even the law cannot evict him easily. Where will those five families go? We have all divided up the colony among ourselves. Do you think anybody will give up their share now? That will just lead to more fighting among ourselves. And that's exactly what those people are after.'

'How can they start a fight between us, if we don't want it? Absolute rubbish.'

'It is the reason that is so important, Dibya. If they can create the reason then fighting is inevitable. Each family now has a small allocation of land. How much can they give up that? Besides, the number of people in the colony is increasing. There are nearly one-and-a-half-times as many now as there were when we first came. So actually, we need more space—giving up space is absurd. And we also need to set up a school here, as well as a playground for the children.'

'Listen, first we have to survive, then we can dream of these luxuries.'

'This is not luxury. We can't live forever like animals in a pen, with food and shelter as our only preoccupations. We have been here for a long time now. It's about time we started to live like human beings.'

'I've had enough of those lectures. You talk big, but none of you can show us the way to such higher living. Well, I'll suggest another thing. Why don't we fill up the pond? That will create a big area of space. I myself will put in labour to fill in the pond.'

The pond, however, was such a live and axiomatic part of the existence of the colony, that this possibility raised a tremendous outcry. The people who lived in the colony were basically rural people, and all their lives they had been used to ponds, not having had the facility of running water. So they had been gratified to find a pond right in the middle of the colony. Besides, it really was a beautiful piece of water, the two banks neatly bound with stone steps, the water deep and pellucid. It never went dry, not even in the high summer. There were no water taps within the colony. You had to go out to the main road to fetch your drinking water from the tubewell there. For every other purpose, the pond was the answer.

Once the excitement had subsided a little, Arjun remonstrated with Dibya.

'How can you even say such a thing, Dibya? You want to make over land to the factory even at the cost of filling in the pond! Can there be an end to such concessions? If you give way once, it will boomerang endlessly. Now they want the five families to move. How do you know that after that they won't demand five more families move? I think that is exactly what they will do. The factory owner is hand in glove with Mr Dutta. We must all get together and resist them. There is no other way. Nobody else is concerned with our real problems. Even the political parties are obsessed with other matters. We don't have voting rights yet, so they won't care too much about us. If we fall apart now, then...'

Sukhen interrupted in a shrill squeak.

'I'm sick and tired of this playing around with words. Did we come here to listen to speeches, or are we going to do something constructive?'

Arjun looked at him coolly. Why were these people changing so rapidly? he wondered. Only a matter of five years ago, the same Sukhen used to play the part of Krishna in the local stage plays. He sang beautifully too. He had not then learned to grind out his words like this. Dibya too was becoming impatient.

'Grandfather,' he said, 'all this talk is not going to get us anywhere. If anybody has anything useful to suggest, let them speak up.'

Grandfather Nishi said, 'But Arjun has not said anything unfair. We have lived together for so long, through so many trials. How can we start quarrelling among ourselves?'

'Then there is no need for me to stay any longer,' said Dibya. 'I have had my say.'

'But what are you saying really? To give up our land?'

'Yes, that's the best alternative from every point of view. That way, we'll keep Kewal Singh on our side, he will help us when we are in trouble.'

'But what about those people whose houses will have to be brought down?'

'Well, they will have to put up with some inconvenience. But we can't all land ourselves in trouble just for a few.'

'You can bring yourself to say a thing like that?'

'Listen, it's fine to talk about other people when you yourself are well provided for. Your son has managed to set up his own shop, you don't have to worry about food and lodging. So you can be full of charity towards others. But what about those who have nobody at home to earn them a living? What about the boys who can't get a job? Who's going to think about them? Kewal Singh has promised to give them jobs in the factory.'

Arjun shook his head sadly at that.

'Dibya, such jobs are quite worthless. They are only the bait being dangled before your eyes. He never offered jobs before.'

'Well, now he has given us jobs and he's promised to hire more of the boys. If he can expand his factory, he will need people, and that will be to our advantage. If a number of people can be helped at the cost of inconveniencing just a few...'

'You mean to say that you are so tempted by jobs that you are asking these "few" to become homeless for a second time?'

'Look, you think you are so smart, you understand everything, don't you? Nobody else has any brains. Let me tell you something. If we don't cooperate with these people, they will simply move their factory out of Bengal. Who stands to gain by that?'

'Dibya, please listen to me...'

But Dibya had already got up.

'I have nothing more to listen to,' he said arrogantly. 'I have had my say, now you all can do just as you please. Come on Sukhen.'

Grandfather Nishi tried to plead with him.

'Please, Dibya, stay a bit more, listen to us. Don't get so excited. After all, you are our main support.'

'I told you. I have had my say.'

Haradhan was staring helplessly at Dibya. He seemed convinced that his house would be pulled down. Fate, it was all fate. There was nothing you could do to fight it. Dhiren Shikdar touched Arjun on the arm, and said in a trembling voice, 'Arjun, do we really have to be thrown out again? Where will I go with my wife and child? Oh merciful Lord!'

Old Nepal Shamanta had had a son killed three or four years ago, at the hands of the police. The boy had joined a gang of wagon-breakers in Ghughudanga station. Ever since, the old man had become somewhat unbalanced. He sat there now, muttering to himself, 'Yes, yes, everything will go now. Houses will be pulled down, not a brick left standing. There will be another Pakistan here.'

The other two of the five families had no adult male members. Three widows, a host of children, and a few boys in their late teens who had no jobs either. There was nobody to speak for them. Arjun came close up to Dibya. He held his hand and spoke in his sincerest tones, 'Dibya, you haven't quite understood yet. This is not just a question of letting your land go. If you ask people who have once lost their home and belongings, to uproot themselves once again, then how do you think they'll feel? It's like pulling up a tree by its roots, the same tree that you once planted with your own hands. I beg of you, please don't be so obstinate.'

Dibya pulled his hand away with some violence.

'Look,' said he, 'I've had more than my fair share of whining. I don't want to hear another word. Come on, you lot...'

Eight or nine boys, Sukhen included, rose. Dibya left the gathering with them, his footsteps resounding on the ground, his breath hissing in anger. There was silence for some time. The older people had been made to realize that it was the young who were going to call the tune. The opinions of their seniors would not count anymore. Dibya's angry departure had left most of them crushed. Haradhan, with a face drained of all colour, cheeks caved in suddenly, started trying to cadge cigarettes off his neighbours.

Grandfather Nishi stretched his arm forward, and called one last time, 'Dibya, are you really leaving? Don't go. Come near me for a minute, please Dibya.'

It was time for Haran to start his day's work with the taxi. He got up and said, 'He's left already, Grandfather. He can't hear you.'

'Why did he have to leave like that? Can't any of you go and call him back?'

'Call him back? Who's going to go after Dibya now? He's absolutely mad with fury.'

'Has Arjun left too?'

Arjun went up to Grandfather Nishi.

'No, I'm still here,' he said. 'You heard everything Grandfather. What would you have us do?'

The old man spoke slowly.

'Well, Arjun, whatever you may think, Dibya was not being entirely unreasonable. The scriptures tell us that in times of danger the wise man is happy to give up half of what he has. If we are to save this colony, we must give up something. I'll talk to Biswanath myself, and persuade him to set aside a portion of our land. If some of the others will only chip in...'

Nobody made any comments. They all sat there silent, their faces averted.

'What are you suggesting Grandfather!' exclaimed Arjun. 'That is not the way to survive. That is the way to defeat, to losing out totally. We still have a chance to organize ourselves and make a stand against them.'

'No, my dear boy, no. If Dibya and his gang go against us, we don't have a leg to stand on. It's best to listen to him.'

'But that means accepting injustice. Why don't you get hold of Dibya alone and talk to him?'

Grandfather looked quite helpless.

'You think he's going to listen to me? When he was a little child, I used to play with him, look after him. His grandfather was my first cousin. But now—oh no, he has no time for me. I beg of you all, don't fight him any longer.'

Arjun turned to face the others. His voice was heavy with deep hurt.

'I don't know if any of you will pay any attention to me. But still, I'll say this. Not one of you should leave your homes. Don't give them an inch of your land, come what may.'

*

At night, Arjun was sitting down to dinner. Shantilata sat nearby, fanning him. Arjun had helped himself to a lot of rice and had mixed it up with the lentils, but he didn't seem to have any appetite at all. There were all the special vegetarian delicacies he loved so much. But he just picked at his food in a half-hearted, dejected manner.

'Why do you look so depressed?' Shantilata asked.

156

'Depressed? Not at all.'

'But you've hardly touched a thing.'

'I am not hungry. I happened to have a snack this afternoon at one of the restaurants.'

'You shouldn't eat all that rubbish they serve you in restaurants.

There was no fish today. Shantilata had cooked some curried eggs. Even though she was herself a widow, and restricted to a vegetarian diet, Shantilata cooked all sorts of non-vegetarian food for her son. She obeyed all the religious instructions and prohibitions for herself, but not for her son. She said again, 'If you don't fancy the lentils, put it aside. Have some rice with the curried eggs.'

Arjun tasted some and said, 'Yes, it's very good.'

'What was that meeting all about today, the one at Biswanath's?'

'Oh, don't let us talk about it mother. I am sick of it all. The rot has set in among us. We are in for even worse times.'

'Don't you get too caught up in all this. You have your work to do.'

'Yes, that's just what I think from time to time. But I just can't stay out. We do not live on an island. The people around us are bound to obtrude on our minds.'

'There are lots of other people in this colony. If they don't have any sense, what can you do all by yourself? Don't keep on being so depressed. My heart sinks if I see that look on your face.'

Arjun feebly tried to smile.

'Don't you fret, Mother. I am all right.'

'I have closed the window. Don't open it again tonight.'

After finishing his meal, Arjun returned to his room and sat in his chair. It wouldn't be a bad idea to have a cigarette. In an old packet in the drawer, Arjun found just one cigarette. What about matches, though. Suddenly he remembered that Shukla had once given him a lighter. A little rummaging around was enough to find it. There was still enough fuel to light it. He contemplated the lighter. It was quite an expensive object, and yet he could leave it lying around carelessly. But there was a time when just a red and blue pencil and a harmonica...Shukla had a habit of giving him little presents from time to time. It would be her birthday soon; she was sure to invite him. She usually invited two to three hundred people for the occasion. It would be nice to give her something then. But what to give her? Whatever you could think of, she already possessed. How do you feel if you give someone a present, and then find that the person already has two or three of those?

Shantilata, having finished all her housework, came to his door and asked, 'Do you need anything else? A glass of water?'

Actually she had come to check whether Arjun had absentmindedly opened the window again.

'No, mother,' said Arjun, 'I don't want anything. I'll come with you now and switch off the light in your room.'

'Don't stay up too late.'

Arjun came back to sit in his room and this time he did open the window. He was not going to be scared into locking himself in. Somebody had reached in through this very window and tried to murder him. He had not hurt anybody, yet somebody had thought it would be advantageous to ensure his removal. But Arjun was not going to die so easily.

He had met Shukla unexpectedly today in Dharmatala. He had been waiting there for the bus, on his way home from the National Library. Suddenly Ranajoy's red two-seater had come up and stopped in front of him. Shukla had put a smiling face out of the window to ask, 'Hello, Becharam's master, what are you waiting for?'

Ever since she had found out that his dog was called Becharam, she had sometimes used that appellation for him.

Arjun had smiled at her.

'Oh, I was just standing here and wondering whether I would meet you.'

'Haven't seen you around the house for a few days. Don't tell me you have given up your research?'

'Even if I do go to your house, it doesn't mean I have to see you, does it?'

'No, but I would have known about your visit. You see, if I don't see you for several days, I miss you, I feel sad.'

And Shukla and Ranajoy had burst into laughter. It was *de rigueur* to laugh like this whenever you talked about being sad. Arjun had smiled with them.

'Well, have you really stopped working?' she had asked again. 'Do we have to believe that you've finally come to your senses?'

'No, I have just been working at the National Library for the last few days.'

'I've never seen anyone like you, Arjun,' Ranajoy had said. 'To carry on work even after you have passed all your exams.'

'And remember,' Shukla had added, 'people who write their theses after slogging so much are not considered brilliant scholars.'

'Oh, I am not brilliant at all. I just cram things into my brain with hard work.'

'Come on, Arjun,' Ranajoy had urged, 'get in. We are going for a Chinese meal.'

'Please excuse me today. You go on.'

Shukla had snapped at him.

'Get in, I tell you. We'll not take no for an answer. You are much too ready to say no to everything.'

Arjun had kept on smiling as he observed the look of mock anger on Shukla's face.

'Once is not enough,' he had said. 'You'll have to order me like that three times, before I come.'

'Stop talking nonsense and just get in.'

'But there is no room in the car. It is so small.'

'Don't worry. We'll make room.'

Shukla had moved closer to Ranajoy, and Arjun had had to crowd in next to her. Ranajoy was almost as handsome as one of the gods of Greek mythology. No cloud of sadness ever touched his face. Next to him, Shukla in her red sari had looked like a living tongue of flame.

'Which place would you prefer, Arjun?' Ranajoy had asked. 'You must tell us. It has to be your choice today.'

'You know how all Chinese men are supposed to look alike. It's the same with Chinese restaurants as far as I am concerned.'

'I knew you were a rustic,' Shukla had said.

The next hour had flown by. No hatred, no envy, no small-minded self interest; only unclouded joy and spurts of laughter. Shukla never allowed anyone to wear a long face when she was around.

Arjun opened a book as he sat there in his room, but he just could not concentrate. It was extremely sultry tonight, he thought. Perhaps it would start raining soon. Some distance away, a bomb exploded. Such sounds were becoming quite common at night these days. Arjun sighed heavily. Who knew what kind of people were preparing what acts of destruction? This kind of solitary explosion was an indication that it was not a part of some conflict, it was just a bomb being tested after manufacture.

He switched off the light and went to bed. How nice it had been to see Shukla today. But some time back he had seen Purnima, from his own colony, near the Victoria Memorial. That was also an evening when he had been walking home from the National Library, but it was later than usual. In one deserted corner of Cathedral Road, two drunken men had been pulling Purnima by both arms in two different directions. A scene of unmistakable vice! And Purnima? She had been laughing hysterically. A policeman had come up to them, and Arjun stopped short had a little way off. Just in case he was needed to help. But he did not have to do anything. Purnima was obviously an old hand at this game, she had an understanding with the police. She had not seemed to be the least bit scared, but had talked to the policeman while laughing in the same hysterical fashion. Arjun had decided to move on, so that Purnima would not see him and feel embarrassed.

What an enormous gulf of distance between Shukla's life and that aspect of Purnima's life. Many young men did pull Shukla by the arm, but there was nothing sordid about it. Nothing repulsive, nor any commitment to sin. Why did Purnima have to descend into this heartless existence of shame and slime?

Arjun decided he was not going to concern himself

with these things anymore. What could he do? Could he be of any help to Purnima.? Or maybe Purnima had deliberately chosen to go that way and did not want help. But what about Labonya? That poor girl was trying so hard, so very hard...

IX

Night was deepening into the dead hours. Labonya was
memorizing a textbook, swaying with her own rhythm.
Her voice sounded like the monotonous crying of a baby.
She could never remember anything by heart, unless she
read aloud. Tomorrow was her chemistry exam, that was
the hardest one. She had thought she would discuss a few
of the important problems with Arjun, but to visit him
now would immediately set tongues wagging. No, she
would pass her exams by herself.

The prolonged session at work had made her back
stiff. She could never stay up after a heavy meal, so her
dinner had been covered and set aside for her. Some of
the girls in her class had said that if you ate bread
instead of rice, you wouldn't feel so sleepy. But Labonya
was from East Bengal, she couldn't stand anything but
rice.

She yawned twice, and stopped reading. She might as
well eat now. The colony was absolutely silent, in all
likelihood not a soul was awake. She peeped out of her
window and saw that even Arjun's window was dark.
Sometimes Arjun*da* would stay up all night to study.

Labonya put aside her books, got off the bed and sat
down on the floor to eat. Cold rice and lentils, curried
vegetables and a broth with some small fish in it.
Labonya's family could not afford to eat fish or meat
every day.' But now that she was taking her exams, she
was given an egg for breakfast and fish for lunch and
dinner. This was just a special arrangement for her.

Labonya smelt the fish broth. There was a slightly sour
smell to it. Obviously, it had gone off a little. Not

162

surprising in this heat. She mixed up all the rice with the lentils, thinking she would not have any of the fish. But she started tasting it a little, and somehow found that she had finished it. She had not been aware of it before, but she was ravenously hungry.

She took her plate with all the leavings and put it out in the courtyard. There was a pailful of water there too. But still, just to shake the sleepiness from her brain, Labonya walked over to the pond to wash her hands. There was a lot of moonlight tonight. It was pleasant to be outside after having sat inside in the oppressive heat. The coconut fronds were absolutely still, not a breath of air anywhere. And even at this unearthly hour, she suddenly heard the sound of a truck going down the road. That, however, was only the exception which emphasized the total silence. The northern corner of the colony, near the nettle bushes, was the common site for dumping the garbage. There was a sudden rustle there—probably a jackal. They did come in from time to time. Arjun's dog, Becharam, ran towards it, barking.

Arjun's brother, Shomnath, had been very attached to that dog. Labonya could still remember Shomnath. How sad it had been to watch him lose his sanity day by day. He never harmed anybody, yet the boys would drive him berserk by throwing stones at him. Labonya had been a child then—she too had joined in the jeering laughter, when Shomnath was seen talking to his dog. A little wave of sadness rose in her heart at the memory. You could never tell when the accumulated grief for a person would suddenly surface. Labonya could never have foreseen that a stroll so late at night, to chase away the fumes of sleep, would lead to heartache for Shomnath.

Labonya, standing on the edge of the pond, started rinsing out her mouth and spitting the water out as far as she could—like a child. In fact, as children, they had always tried to compete with each other—who could spit the water out furthest. The pond was calm and motionless. At night even familiar water looked so mysterious. She played with water for a long time. Sprinkled some over her face, neck and breast. Her body started feeling cool again.

The footsteps startled her. She quickly readjusted her sari and turned around. Sukhen was coming down the steps on the bank, terror evident on his entire face. It looked as though somebody had tried to strangle him, his eyes were almost popping out of his head. Between gasps for breath he said, 'Labi, something terrible has happened. Absolute disaster. Somebody has again come and beaten Arjun up.'

A hammer seemed to start pounding violently on her heart.

The blood draining out of her face, Labonya asked, 'Again? Oh no! Where is he?'

She glanced back for an instant towards Arjun's room; the window was open into the darkness inside.

'They have left him lying near the rubbish dump,' said Sukhen. 'He's probably dead this time.'

But Labonya had started running before he had finished speaking. Arjun's dog too had been running in that direction, she recalled. She reached the spot before Sukhen. She had just bent forward to the ground, when two figures materialized out of the darkness, covered her face, lifted her in their arms and started running. Labonya tried kicking with her arms and legs, to release herself. But the suddenness of the attack left her helpless in their grip.

In the open courtyard of the plywood factory, sat Dibya, on a wooden stool. Several other people sat on the ground. Kewal Singh himself was not present, but there were a couple of men from the factory. Several bottles were visible, bones lay scattered all over the place.

Sukhen said with a grin, 'My God, she certainly gave us trouble. Not an easy one to get hold of. I told her Dibya that you wanted to speak to her. And you know what she said? "Do you think I'll go running just because Dibya*da* wants me? Let him come here. I don't give a damn for your great Dibya." '

The two men had put Labonya down on the ground, but they still held her firmly by both arms as she stood there. She was not a girl to lose her nerve easily, and she tried now to make a quick assessment of the situation. Apart from Dibya and Sukhen, there were two or three other young men from the colony. They too wore an unnatural expression. They too were hungering for flesh. These boys were the same age as herself, but had never become her friends, never cared for her. They had only raked her with lustful, covetous glances.

Dibya was puffing away at his cigarette, his eyes unnaturally bloodshot. With his stupendously powerful physique—in his present intoxicated state, he was terrifying. Labonya turned and looked at Sukhen and reproached him with spirit.

'Aren't you ashamed to lie, you wizened little monkey? We'll see what happens to you tomorrow morning. You'll get what is coming to you.'

'You hear that Dibya? Just look at her, the insolent bitch.'

Dibya spoke then. His voice was surprisingly calm. First, he ordered the two men to release Labonya. Then he said, 'Sit down Labi. I have something to say to you.'

'Why should I? I have my exams tomorrow.'

'Just give me five minutes. I have only a couple of things to discuss with you.'

'Well, can't you come to my house and talk to me there? Who's ever stopped you from coming? Dibya*da*, is this what you have come down to? God, you people make me sick!'

'Don't be afraid. Nobody will do anything to you. You'll go home in a minute...'

'Of course, I shall. Who's going to stop me? You think I am scared of you and your lot?'

'Softly, softly. There's no need to shout.'

'Why not? For fear of you?'

Sukhen could contain himself no longer.

'I told you, Dibya, I told you what she was like. You see how she answers back? And you must know how she gets the nerve to do that.'

Dibya, however, did not lose his cool. A strange smile flitted over his face. It was never possible to predict what Dibya would choose to do or not do. Many people had been astounded by his acts of magnanimity or cruelty at unexpected moments. He smiled again, with satisfaction.

'Good, very good,' he said. 'I like to see a girl with some spirit. It's women who really run the world. What were you thinking of doing after your exams, Labi?'

'Is this why you dragged me over here at this time of night? To ask me this?'

Sukhen could be heard muttering through his teeth.

'As if you would come of your own accord, if we hadn't brought you by force? I know your sort. Nothing without trouble from you.'

Labonya heard him, and started trembling with anger. Her whole body expressed her contempt for Sukhen as she looked at him.

'Dibya*da*,' she said, 'don't let him say another word.'

'Yes, she's right. Shut up, Sukhen.'

'I'll tell everybody in the colony tomorrow morning,' said Labonya. 'If they don't do something about this, I'll call in the police. Do you really think you can hold me here by force?'

'You will leave this place any moment now, and completely free. No one will say anything to you. But let me just make one request Labi. This poor fool, Sukhen, is always whining because you won't marry him. Why do you treat him like dirt? A spirited wife like you—that's exactly what Sukhen needs.'

Labonya's eyes flashed fire. With immense contempt she said, 'What! Marry that creature! If he ever dares come close to me, I'll gouge his eyes out.'

All the other men burst out in loud, raucous laughter. Sukhen suddenly ran forward and slapped Labonya hard on the cheek.

'You bitch,' he ground out viciously through his teeth, 'you think only Arjun is good enough for you, do you? We'll settle that today for good.'

Though the suddenness of the attack had stunned Labonya, she did manage to recover and was about to push Sukhen away, when Dibya came over, took him by the scruff of his neck and knocked him over like a small child. Then he gave Sukhen a savage kick and said, 'You son of a bitch. You dare lay hands on a girl from our colony in front of me.'

The others also echoed the sentiment.

'Yes, by God, this is too much. Lay hands on a woman! Just like that damned Sukhen...'

Dibya laid his hand affectionately on Labonya's shoulder.

'Labi,' he said, 'please don't object any longer. Please marry that idiot, Sukhen. He just goes on and on about you, that he loves you a lot. He really does, too. Tonight, for instance. We were just sitting here, all of us, enjoying our drinks—and there he was moaning about you. That was why I told him to go and fetch you. I promised to talk to you.'

'You think I'll marry him just because you tell me so? I'd rather poison myself.'

'Why must you get so worked up? Think it over carefully. Sukhen is not such a bad fellow. And since he wants you so badly—you know he refuses to marry anybody else—I only want what is best for you, Labi dear.'

'Dibya*da*, how can you do this to me? How can you force me so unjustly?'

Dibya suddenly seemed to change his mind.

'Force? Am I forcing you? Very well, go home then. We'll talk some other time.'

As Labonya still kept on standing there he said again, 'What are you waiting for? Go home—get back to your books.'

Labonya started to back off, step by slow step. Sukhen had sat up by then, and was gaping at her. Dibya bent his head and took a swig from his glass. Then he raised his face and spoke quietly.

'Just remember one thing,' he said. 'This habit of yours, of running to Arjun every so often for advice— this won't do you any good. Has Arjun told you not to marry Sukhen?'

'No, of course not! How does Arjun*da* come into all this? Why should he say any such thing, anyway?'

'But that is what Sukhen tells me all the time.'

'You tell him never even to mention Arjun*da's* name. He isn't worth as much as Arjun*da's* little toe.'

'Listen, Labi. We all know that you've lost your head completely over Arjun. But let me tell you just one little thing. Arjun is not going to have any say in the affairs of this colony any more. I am going to get rid of him.'

'Why, what harm has he done you?'

'He's too thick with those West Bengalis. Well then, let him go and live with them. What has he ever done for this colony? Just a lot of big talk! And always obstructing us. I am going to teach him a good lesson.'

'Dibyada, you never used to be like this before. It's this crowd here that is dragging you down so low. And that Punjabi fellow too, he's turned your head.

'Be quiet! It's Arjun who's put all these ideas into your head. Sukhen is right. You think Arjun can save you? What is he worth, anyway? Just look at him. If you hit him once, there's no more room to hit him again. Ever since I was a boy, all I hear everybody talking about is "Arjun" and "Arjun". As if he is out of this world. Maybe he's got a few degrees—so what? Go and survey the streets of Calcutta, and you'll find scores of degree holders wandering around with nothing to do. When Arjun starts looking for a job, he'll find that out for himself. We here, are trying to do something for the general good of the colony—but he has to come and interfere there too. Well, I've had my fill of him. This time I won't let him off.'

'Why are you saying this to me? You sit down and work it out with him. What do I know of such matters?'

'I order you to marry Sukhen. And remember, never speak to Arjun again, never. I'll tell your father also.'

'You really believe you can order me around?'

Dibya lunged forward and grabbed one of her wrists. But Labonya immediately snatched it back with some force. In bitter tones she said, 'What do you think you are doing? You think you can get away with anything with brute force. You think I'll stop speaking to Arjunda by your orders?

When she became angry, Labonya completely lost her head. Even after she had been forced to come here at dead of night, she might have had a chance to escape, if only she had appealed to Dibya's better feelings. But at this point she had become one consuming flame of anger. All fear had evaporated out of her system. Otherwise she would have remembered that it was never wise to use phrases like 'brute force' in front of Dibya. If there was one thing he could not stand, it was slighting references to his physical strength.

Having said those words, Labonya looked into Dibya's eyes, and for the first time she was afraid, deadly afraid. She started backing off fast, at once, but Dibya said in a completely different voice, 'Grab that girl.'

Labonya started running for dear life. Dibya loped forward in pursuit like a huge tiger. Labonya could run fast. But can the swiftest doe ever escape the pursuing tiger?

When Dibya finally grabbed hold of her hair at the northern corner of the pond, Labonya screamed. It is hardly possible that no one in the neighbouring house heard that scream. But just as with the unholy scream of a disembodied spirit in the watches of the night—no one was willing to acknowledge that sound. Or if they did, they were not prepared to risk venturing outside.

The instant before Dibya clamped his hand over her mouth, Labonya pleaded desperately, 'Dibyada, dear 'Dibyada, I beg of you. I am like your own sister, please...'

Her sari had fallen off her shoulder. A momentary slackening of grip enabled her to run forward again, her whole body trembling now with whimpering tears. But Dibya's enormous fist came and caught her blouse at the back. Blood was running from her mouth but still Labonya had not given in. As soon as she got the chance she bit Dibya in the arm with all her strength. The agony made him slacken his embrace a little, and she was off again. But Dibya fell on the ground and tripped Labonya with his outstretched leg.

She was still making an attempt to roll forward along the ground, when Dibya settled his whole enormous weight on her and said, 'So, it's only Arjun who's going to enjoy your body, eh?'

'Dibyada, I beg of you, I have my exams tomorrow. Don't ruin me like this.'

'Go and complain to Arjun. We'll see what he can do.'

'Dibyada let me go, please let me go. I beg of you.'

'Shut up! You have the nerve to talk back to me, you little...'

'You are hurting me, hurting me! Help!'

Labonya was trying to resist him with all her strength, scratching, biting, kicking. She rolled about frantically on the ground, but to Dibya with his tremendous strength, she was like a brittle toy. As she opened her mouth to scream again, Dibya pressed his left hand over her mouth and hit her hard on the neck with his right. A grunt escaped Labonya, she threshed about for a few seconds like an injured animal and was still.

Dibya's companions stood watching from a distance. The moonlight had been gone for some time. In the murky darkness, they looked like an array of ghosts. If someone from one of the houses had opened a window and seen them, he wouldn't have been able to sleep for fear.

A little while later, Dibya got up and came towards them, swaying on his feet. In his harshest voice he said, Come on you bastards. 'What are you staring at?'

They went into the courtyard of the factory.

After an interval, Sukhen stealthily came out again. He knelt on the ground and whimpered, 'Labi, Labi, get up. Get up and go home. I am sorry, Labi. Please forgive me. I'll never again...'

The blood still trickled down the corner of her mouth. She did not stir. Her hair fell all over her face. Sukhen nudged her again.

'Get up Labi, go home. Please forgive me. This will never happen again. Why did you have to provoke Dibya? You should know he gets angry when provoked like that. Please get up. You have your exams to take tomorrow. I'll never bother you again, never ever. Do forgive me.'

Sukhen was crying. But there was no depth to his emotions, even at this moment. For when he found that he could not make Labonya move, even after a few efforts, he smelt danger. Like a wary fox, he looked around carefully and disappeared once more.

Shortly after that, it began to rain. Drizzles of water poured all over Labonya's motionless body.

X

Several incidents took place in the colony within a few days of each other.

On the day of her chemistry examination, Labonya fainted away in the hall. She suddenly stopped writing, put her elbows on the table and covered her face. Then came loud, tumultuous sobs. She just could not remember any of the answers. All the other girls stopped writing, the invigilators came running, but Labonya could not say one word in reply to their enquiries. As soon as somebody touched her, she just fainted dead away.

She had not said anything to her family at home, had not shed a single tear—except during the examinations—and that too because she could not remember the answers. She never cried after that.

Some people from the examination centre took Labonya home. She had still not recovered. It was not possible for her to take the rest of the exams. The BSc exams that she had set her heart on passing, remained incomplete this time too.

The next few days she suffered from very high fever and constant delirium. And all of that delirium centred on death.

'Kill me, kill me, why couldn't you have killed me outright?' Or 'I am dead already. Hell lies around me. Ohhhh! I burn all over, Mother, I'm on fire!'

Once she recovered from this bout of illness, Labonya relapsed into total silence. As if she had suddenly lost her speech. Not a word did she have for anybody. Arjun went to visit her twice, but she would not speak to him.

Labonya's parents were completely crushed by this catastrophe. Biswanath had already had a grievance against the world. Now the cloud never lifted from his face. He felt this was just part of a plot against him. His eldest son had died after coming of age. This daughter could perhaps have helped support the family if only she had got her degree. They were all doubly scared because there seemed to be indications of insanity in Labonya's behaviour now. A poor family burdened with an insane daughter for the rest of their life! So they started making all possible efforts to arrange a marriage for her.

Arjun felt really depressed about Labonya. The girl had wanted to be good, to rise above her surroundings—and she had failed. How can one measure the immensity of sorrow behind that failure? But who knows, perhaps one day she would be able to forget everything. Arjun had told Biswanath that he was prepared to take Labonya for consultation to Abanish's father. But it was Labonya who refused to go. She was adamant. She kept on looking at Arjun with burning reproach in her eyes. As if it was Arjun who had done her some grievous wrong. Arjun finally made up his mind that he was not going to let all these things bother him. It was not in his power to help. What good was he to poor Labonya?

Arjun redoubled his efforts at concentrating on his work. He hardly ever went out. Shukla had been right in saying that it was useless to carry on with academic work after getting a Master's degree. Abanish had persuaded him to undertake this research, but maybe it would have been better not to have. It would be such a relief to get it over and done with. His grant was also due to run out. So Arjun borrowed a typewriter from Abanish and clattered away at it night and day, typing his thesis.

Kewal Singh had started taking a short cut through the colony now. Formerly, there was hardly an outsider who could enter the colony. In the very early days there were some pimps who had haunted the neighbourhood, on the lookout for healthy, young refugee girls. Then the boys had banded together one day and chased them off with sticks; they had never been seen since then. But now,

Kewal Singh had already employed two or three of the colony boys. He had certainly acquired special status.

Kewal Singh's designs on the land occupied by the five houses had intensified now. He had managed to land an order worth nearly three million rupees, to supply plywood chests for storing tea. But he was finding it impossible to supply the goods on time, without expanding the factory.

Meanwhile, the people in the colony got embroiled in frequent arguments over whether to accept Kewal Singh's proposal or not. The sons of households living outside the coveted territory were prepared to override all objections in the hope of getting jobs in the factory. Nothing seemed sweeter to their ears than the assurances of a job. If every one of them got employed, even at the cost of transforming the whole colony into a factory and a barrack, perhaps even that would be quite acceptable to them.

On the other hand, there were the people like Haradhan or Dhiren Shikdar, who just could not come to a unanimous decision. So they kept coming back to Arjun.

'What shall we do, Arjun? You tell us. We just can't cope with these people any longer.'

Arjun would try to maintain his detachment.

'I have nothing to say. It's your land and your household. So you must decide what is best.'

'But we just don't understand anything. That Dibya has now gone over to their camp. Can anybody survive here after flouting him? What shall we do now, where are we to go? Who will give us shelter? All the others in the colony have refused to help us out and part with their land. Can't you submit a petition to the government?'

'I don't know the language of petitions, Uncle,' replied Arjun.

'Of course, you do. You are the only one who can do something like that. Don't you even know some ministers?'

'Listen, I don't even know the orderlies of the ministers. Even they are more important people than I am.'

'That Punjabi fellow has been tempting us with an

offer of a thousand rupees per family. Maybe in the end, we'll just get nothing. Do you think it is a wise move to give in now and take the money?'

'Do, if you feel like that.'

'But Arjun, where shall we live after we've taken the money?'

'Uncle, please. Why do you think I have the answer to everything? How can I tell you where to live? Perhaps with that money you can rent rooms in the slums.'

'Rent rooms! How long will the money last anyway? And you ask us to go to the slums—with all those ill-begotten, low-caste people?'

'Then maybe you can try another tack. There's a new wave of refugees coming in these days. Why don't you go and mingle with them, and lie down on the platform at Sealdah station? The government will send you to a camp in Dandakaranya or Mana—you will also get cash doles.'

Dhiren Shikdar's eyes brimmed over with tears. Haradhan stared at him helplessly and out of sheer habit, picked up Arjun's packet of cigarettes, and put it in his own pocket. Then Dhiren wiped his eyes.

'Arjun,' he said, 'is this what we have to hear even from you? You were the main source of our strength. We have been together here for so long now, all of us sharing our joys and our sorrows. And now Kewal Singh can just come and evict us while the rest of you don't say a word in protest? Even if we have to die, we had hoped it would be while we were together. That's all we had hoped for...'

Arjun got up.

'Look,' said he, 'I have already told you what I think. If you listen to me, then not one of you must give up an inch of your land. Never, and never.'

Arjun was perpetually despondent these days. This problem was gnawing away at him, yet he could find no way out of the impasse. What hurt him most was the fact that the unity among the members of the colony had been destroyed. Even Grandfather Nishi, whose wisdom had been generally relied upon, was unwilling to go against Dibya any longer.

Arjun had stopped going to visit Shukla's room when he was over at Abanish's. He felt he just could not fit into the carefree, happy world inhabited by Shukla. The people with whom he had spent all these years, starting from the days of trudging on foot from Jessore, these people were confronted by the ultimate crisis—and yet, he, Arjun, could do nothing.

Abanish asked him one day, 'What is the matter, Arjun? Why do you seem so preoccupied these days? Have you fallen in love or what?'

Arjun could not give him a ready answer, he just gave him a pale, lifeless smile. What was the use of talking to Abanishda about their domestic problems? He had received plenty of favours from Abanishda. What was the point of embarrassing him with more problems? Yet, finally, he could not help coming out with it.

Abanish did not quite grasp the implications of the whole business. He had never had to bother with the minor details of land ownership. But he was willing to help.

'I have a friend,' he said, 'in the Refugee Rehabilitation Department. He is probably the deputy director now. Why don't you go and see him? Just in case it helps.'

But the visit was entirely fruitless. Mr Chakrabarty of Refugee Rehabilitation was a *pucca sahib*. He hardly spoke anything but English. Abanish had told him all about Arjun in his letter of introduction. So, since this was an academic person, there was no point in not showing off his command over English.

Had it been at any other time, Arjun would have never allowed a person like this escape without a barbed comment or two, however indirect. But his present mood was totally different. After all, he had come to ask for help. Not that Mr Chakraborty did not try to help. He sent for the file from the assistant, the assistant then called in his superior officer, the officer sent for the person in charge of the reference section, who in turn called the record supplier—finally it transpired that the record supplier had gone out for his tea break. Then Mr Chakraborty gave Arjun tea as well, and in the course of the conversation even raised the subject of the war in Vietnam. Why should he let slip this opportunity to show off the range of his knowledge to this boy who had stood first in the MSc examinations? Not only that, he also informed Arjun of all his friends and relatives who had done well at the university, at some time or other.

At last the file appeared, Mr Chakraborty frowned.

'Oh yes, another unauthorized colony. Negotiations are still going on with the landlord. As soon as the matter of the compensation can be finalized—I assure you, it won't take much longer...The central government is putting pressure on us to finalize everything within the year. It's just a matter of the landlord accepting the amount—and he must accept, sooner or later. Immediately after that, you will get the right of possession. In fact, my dear sir, a lot of refugees are getting hold of good land in this way. There was that colony in Anwar Shah Road, which has just been authorized. Just think of the price of land in that area!'

'Yes,' said Arjun, 'but what if someone tries to evict us before we have acquired rights?'

Mr Chakraborty burst into hearty, expansive laughter.

'Who's going to evict you? Does anyone dare to antagonize the refugees these days? I know what pig-headed characters they can be. Sorry, I didn't mean to...'

Arjun realized clearly that since the government had been taking steps to pay out the compensation money to the landlords, the latter were trying to get back as much of their land as possible before the event—by fair means or foul. For the recovered land could be sold off at high prices. This would not be possible in colonies where there was unity among the residents. But if people like Kewal Singh could be roped in to sow dissension...

'Suppose somebody does try to evict us,' said Arjun, 'what then? Can you help us?'

'If the matter is within our purview.'

Then in the sibilant accents of one exchanging secrets, Mr Chakraborty came out with his ideas.

'Look, what good is it, fighting like dogs over small portions of land here? In the end it comes down to Bengalis depriving other Bengalis. Look at all these businessmen from the other provinces of India—they are buying up all the good land available in Calcutta, while the Bengalis are skirmishing among themselves. I have nothing against you in this respect, for after all, you are a scholar. But, why don't you try to persuade the other members of your colony to migrate to Madhya Pradesh or Rajasthan? If only they'd agree, I'll make all the arrangements. The refugees of Bengal should make every effort to occupy as much land as possible in the other provinces. And this is the time to do so. And another thing. Of course this is entirely between the two of us, you realize—but I personally would be happy to see less congestion around the immediate neighbourhood of Calcutta. So if these people are willing to move I can always...'

Arjun felt like breaking in and saying, 'Suppose you were asked to leave your home in Calcutta and go and cultivate land in the jungles of Madhya Pradesh—would you go? If not, then why are you making all these big speeches? Are these people beggars or the objects of your charity?'

But, of course, he did not say anything like that. He had not come here to have an argument. But he also realized clearly that at this point of time he would receive no concrete assistance from this quarter.

He returned home extremely dejected.

'Mother,' he said, 'let's go away from this colony. I just don't like it here anymore.'

Shantilata was considerably taken aback.

'Go! Where to?'

'Anywhere. Suppose I get a flat near the university.'

Shantilata spoke slowly.

'Well, if you really think that's the best idea, then we shall go. But don't do anything on a moment's impulse.'

'No, it's not an impulse. I've made up my mind. I'll start looking for a place tomorrow.'

Somehow, Kewal Singh managed to find out that Arjun had been to the Refugee Rehabilitation Department. For, the next day, he made a sarcastic comment about it as Arjun walked past him. Obviously, they were making it their business to keep abreast of everything.

XI

Two days after this, there was a fire in the colony. Only in the five houses that were the object of contention, and at the same time.

Arjun's family had had to leave their country when their house had been set on fire. Once again, Arjun saw that fire. He was awakened in the middle of the night by a tremendous din. He looked out and saw the houses on the other side of the pond burning furiously. At first, in the disoriented amazement of awakening, Arjun was not sure of what was happening. It looked like the end of the world. Then he rushed out of the house without even a shirt on.

Obviously, no culprits for arson would ever be found. The plywood factory was barred and locked, not a soul was stirring, not even their night watchman. Dibya had gone to Durgapur on factory business, a couple of days ago. And everyone knew it too. As for Sukhen, he had simply disappeared for the last two weeks. No one knew where he was.

Yet, it was evident that these five houses could not have caught fire together, in this uniform fashion, if petrol or kerosene had not been poured over them. The flames were raging in a vast unbroken sheet. All attempts at putting them out were in vain. The problem was that the people could not work in an orderly, disciplined manner. Arjun had made an effort to organize a chain of helpers, passing buckets of water from the pond. But they all started running around together in such a way that nothing remained organized.

Within minutes the houses were reduced to a pile of

ashes. The residents did not have much in the way of possessions, and from that even less was salvaged. There was no loss of life, of course, but Dhiren Shikdar's only son got both his legs badly burnt. Purnima, after rushing out of the house, went back in again in the vain hope of saving some of her saris. But the flames drove her back and she was so scared of the possible damage to her beauty that she burst into loud lamentation. So much so, that finally, she too was sent to the hospital with Dhiren's son.

The whole colony buzzed with loud voices and bitter weeping. East Bengalis can neither speak nor weep quietly—everything is done at the top of their voices. As news of the fire spread, people came rushing over from distant places. An all-night show had been organized in the Nager Bazar area, but even the spectators there had abandoned the show to come and observe the fiery spectacle.

In the early hours of the morning, the Commissioner of the Municipality as well as the Member of the Legislative Assembly, came by with their henchmen. Before leaving, these great men were profuse in their assurances of forcing the government to pay adequate compensation to the deprived families. The local MP had a reputation for great generosity. He was stationed in Delhi at the moment, but his representatives were not slow to appear either, nor were they backward about promising funds from the MP's personal treasury—two hundred rupees per family.

The residents in the neighbouring houses started the usual murmur, of the refugees being habitually filthy, large numbers herding together in one scanty room, not being very sanitary, lighting fires and cooking in the bedrooms—indeed, one should be grateful, they said, that the fire had not spread all over the neighbourhood. But later in the day, these same people were generous enough to take out a subscription among themselves and send provisions over for the distressed families.

All five families had sought shelter in the dance hall, the only concrete building in the colony. There was hardly room to move. There were no stairs to climb to the roof. So, a ladder was fixed up to let some people stay on the roof. Even Arjun's room was full of people. He had packed up all his important books and papers and shoved them under the bed. But he felt totally dispirited. He could see through the whole ruse, but what could he do?

Dibya came back the next day, around ten o'clock in the morning. He was returning from Durgapur. He wore the khaki uniform given out by the factory to its employees. He had been hired as the 'caretaker,' a reasonably important position. With his fair complexion and well-muscled body, the khaki unifrom made him look like a soldier from the British army in the colonial days.

He had heard everything, of course, as soon as he set foot inside the colony, and his whole face was overcast with gloom. He started walking towards his own home to change out of his uniform, two of his cronies with him. As soon as Arjun saw Dibya, he stepped down from the porch and came up to him. Holding him by the arm, Arjun said, 'You see how it is, Dibya. Didn't I tell you what would happen if we did not stick together?'

Dibya pulled his hand away and said in a hard, low voice, 'It's because of you that this has happened. It's because of you that so many people don't have a roof over their heads.'

'Because of me?'

'What else? You instructed them not to shift their homes. If they had not listened to you, they might have got some money, at least have saved their belongings.'

Arjun just could not control himself any longer. In an almost deafening voice, he said, 'But why the hell should they have to move their houses? What do you think is going on? Everybody else can stay undisturbed, but those poor people have to move, eh? You think you can get away with this kind of anarchy?'

Dibya maintained his calm.

'Why are you shouting at me? I don't like people to raise their voice in front of me.'

'Dibya, please, you can still reconsider everything. If you step in even now, to take the side of these people, to help them...'

180

'Why drag me into all this? I know nothing about this.'

Shantilata stood on the porch and saw Dibya and Arjun speaking to each other. She could not hear a word, but some ominous fear gripped her heart.

All the elder members of the five families were still overwhelmed by the disaster, and sat on in silence. The women would still burst into racking sobs from time to time, the children rummaged among the pile of ashes and rubble in the hopes of finding something. Suddenly, the children all came back screaming and clamouring. Apparently, a lot of men had turned up at the spot where the houses had burned down and had driven them away.

Arjun, accompanied by Kartik, Kanai and Bishweshwar, went over to investigate. The older men also followed. A totally different scene met their eyes. About ten or eleven workmen had started building a wall with old bricks and mortar. Others were cleaning up the ashes and burnt earth, and uprooting trees from the gardens. All of them were being supervised by Kewal Singh himself and there were two police constables with guns. Work was progressing rapidly—already the wall was knee-high.

'What's going on?' Arjun asked Kewal Singh.

Kewal Singh stroked his beard gravely.

'I have leased this portion of land from Mr Dutta,' he replied. 'It's effectively my land now, I find it unoccupied, so I am building a wall.'

Kartik was one of those whose house had been burnt down.

'You bastard,' he burst out, 'how dare you say this is your land?'

This time Kewal Singh came back at him fiercely.

'Shut your mouth, you fool. Do you think it's your land?'

Formerly, Kewal Singh had always employed the technique of being friendly and pleasant to the people of the colony. Now he had no hesitation about baring his fangs in public. For he had acquired the right of might. Even to the extent of police protection.

'But,' said Arjun, 'how can you think you'll get away with this sort of thing? Burning down their houses in

181

order to acquire land? Do you really believe there is no law in the country?'

Kewal Singh looked with vicious hatred at Arjun. His eyes also expressed a kind of contempt. If this boy had stopped meddling, then he could have gained possession of all this land in a peaceful manner. He would have saved more money too. But here was this Communist, who had managed to read a few books and...

'Careful now, careful of what you say, young fellow. Don't shoot off your mouth before you know your facts. Did I set fire to these houses or did you? Who can say whether you did it or not? If you are so fond of the law, why don't you go to court?'

Arjun saw indeed that it was no use bickering with this man. He must keep his head. The whole thing was such a preposterous, incredible piece of injustice, that it could not possibly go on. There had to be a way out of this.

'Please stop work on this wall,' he said to Kewal Singh. 'I shall go myself to the police station.'

'Go wherever you want to. But why the hell should I stop work? First go and get an order from the police.'

Arjun did not even take the time to have a bath or get something to eat. He just set off for the police station with a few of the others. He came back almost three hours later. The station was quite a distance from the colony, and it was always full of people. Besides, Arjun had not armed himself with a letter from some big shot, which was why he had not been given much attention at first. For quite some time, nobody would even listen to him. Finally, he was forced to burst into a heated tirade, all in English. Everyone present was a Bengali, yet you could never command attention unless you spoke in English. Otherwise, a young man of twenty-five or twenty-six, like himself, was only fit to be a criminal. If he turned up at a police station to lodge a complaint, then it was proper to treat him with considerable disbelief and disrespect. But to carry on speaking in English— well now, that was something different. Anybody who could speak such faultless English, for such a length of time, had to be listened to.

A middle-aged inspector was sent out to conduct an

investigation. To have managed to come back in a police car, accompanied by policemen, restored Arjun's prestige in the colony to some extent. Only Arjun could have done that, could have talked to the police on equal terms, without being intimidated. He had received his diploma from the hands of the President of India himself, so everybody in the police force must know him!

By that time, however, the wall was chest-high. All the rubble had been cleared away. The people of the colony were watching, still stunned by recent events. The inspector was very polite and pleasant. He listened to what both sides had to say with serious attention. First, he spoke to the refugees, asking them some questions. There was no dearth of sympathy in his manner towards them either. He even volunteered the information that a cousin of his had married a girl from East Bengal, and that this girl was a wonderful person. Many of his colleagues also happened to be from East Bengal.

He even bestirred himself to the extent of personally testing the bricks and mortar of the new wall. Then he sat in the courtyard of the plywood factory and listened to Kewal Singh's side of the story. Looked at all his documents. He even refused the cold drinks brought out for him by Kewal Singh. And when he wanted a cigarette, he took one out of his own pack.

After having looked everything over, he spoke to Arjun.

'My dear sir, you are an educated person. You should have realized that this case does not fall within our jurisdiction at all. We cannot make a federal offence out of this. It is all in connection with land ownership. You can take this to court for a civil case. You are saying that five families in the colony had their houses here. But that man has some predated lease documents, saying that this land has been leased to him over the last ten years. So one will have to find out the exact area of the original property, whether this particular portion of land is part of it or not, how many families of refugees live here, where their valid papers are—and all sorts of other details.'

'But how can you ignore such a glaring lie like this

and...'

'Listen, go and get hold of a good lawyer. Prove that this is a lie. Go to court. Building the wall can be stopped only if you get an injunction from court. Apart from that, if you are prepared to name somebody as being responsible for arson, you can lodge a complaint against him with us. But it is already too late, as all the evidence has been cleared away.'

Before leaving, the inspector patted Arjun on the shoulder.

'You are a bright young man,' he said, 'if you ever need any help in the future, please don't hesitate to call on us.'

The man was a very skilful actor. He was not going to let on that he and his police station had already come to a secret arrangement with Kewal Singh.

Arjun knew quite well that it was useless to go to court. Even a child could tell you as much. The refugees had been staying in the colony in the hopes of getting the government to acknowledge its moral responsibility and give them support. But the government had not done anything yet. Nobody had any legal documents proving rights to the property. There could be no case in court without proper deeds and documents. You could appeal to the human feelings of some individual, but the law was completely uninvolved. There was no room for feeling there. Beside, one had to remember, the right to legal redress was a very expensive right—not for the poor. A civil case never took less than three or four years.

In spite of this, however, the importunings of the senior members of the colony forced Arjun to go to a lawyer for advice. He did not feel like continuing these efforts, yet there seemed to be no way to avoid them. He just felt exhausted.

They spent a lot of time at the house of the most prestigious lawyer in the neighbourhood. The gentleman himself could not give them any specific hopes or reassurance, but he went into a detailed discussion of the problem, since he was hoping to contest the forthcoming elections. And, in discussion, his enthusiasm knew no bounds. In his opinion, you could never look at one or two incidents like this in isolation. You had to come to grips with the very basics of the refugee problem.

'That's all very well,' said Arjun, 'but before that, we must find a way for these poor people to survive.'

'But that is exactly what I am trying to say. If you cannot solve the fundamental problem, then you cannot do anyone any good. This is what's wrong with the government. Incidents like this happen—and the government provides short-term immediate assistance and the whole thing is forgotten. Well, I'll try to get a friend of mine to raise this in the Assembly. But even that will take some time.'

Arjun had noticed that it was the fashion to talk about the 'fundamental problem'. It was a wonderful method of salving your conscience. If a man lay dying of starvation in the streets, nobody came forward to help him. Everybody would start talking about the fundamental reason behind poverty in India, the need to remove the fundamental reason first, to change the whole system first, etc. In the meantime the man would simply die.

It was late at night when they got back from the lawyer's. The whole colony was as silent as a graveyard. Only the dance hall seemed like a small boat full of distressed people, floating in mid-ocean. Already, Haran had had words with one of those crowding into the hall. He was not prepared to let so many extra people crowd into his space. The rain kept falling with monotonous regularity—the unfortunates who had taken shelter on the roof kept on getting drenched.

When Arjun and his companions returned, Shantilata was not to be found at home. She had quietly gone out without a word to anyone. She stood underneath the lychee tree for a long time, gazing at the lighted window of a particular house. After some time, Dibya emerged. Now he was back in his khaki uniform—obviously he was going out to work on the night shift.

Even when he came face to face with Shantilata, Dibya tried to avoid her, but Shantilata stopped him, saying, 'Dibya, I've been waiting here to say a few things to you. Will you give me two minutes?'

Dibya stopped in his tracks.

'What is it *Khurima*?'

185

'You must be going to work. Am I making you late?'

'No. no. You go ahead.'

'Dibya, my dear boy, what has gone so wrong between you and Arjun? Are you angry with him?'

There was a short pause, before Dibya answered.

'Khurima, why don't the two of you just leave this colony? The sooner the better for everyone.'

'But why? Why do you say this? We have all been together for so long. Where can I go now?'

'Arjun has become different. We have nothing in common any longer. So it's better for him not to stay here anymore.'

'Please listen to me, Dibya. Arjun is like your younger brother. Don't you remember how you used to play together as children? Aren't you supposed to look after him in times of trouble?'

'Khurima, those days are gone forever. Arjun has changed a lot. I tell you, he and I just don't see eye to eye. on anything'

'What do you mean, changed? He's just as much the boy he used to be.'

'I think you should definitely go away from this place. That will be best for all of us?'

'But where to?'

'You have the means to make a move. Arjun's income will be sufficient to take care of both of you elsewhere. So why should you stay here among these wretched people? Troubles will not stop here very easily. But there is no reason for Arjun to get involved. You might as well leave now, and go live somewhere else.'

'It's not so easy to leave just because you ask us to. I don't know any other people or place here—you all are the only people I know and have known for so long. Think of me a little! How can I dream of going and settling down in some strange place?'

'But there just isn't room in this colony for both myself and Arjun. It's 'either him or me.'

Shantilata's heart missed several beats. She quickly took hold of Dibya's hand. It was completely dark where he was standing. A little light filtered through only to fall on Shantilata's face—a light like sadness.

'Why do you say such a terrible thing?' she said. 'Am I to go mad? To think that you could bring yourself to say such a thing to me! Don't you call me *Khurima*? Your mother's been dead and gone for so long, but just think of her once. I have been like a mother to you also. There have been so many times when I...'

'I've told you already, just leave this place, the two of you. That will be the best thing to do.'

'Very well, we shall go then. But it will take a little time. And you, you must promise me that no harm shall come to Arjun. Promise.'

'If Arjun concerns himself only with his work, his books and his research, no one will lay a finger on him. Nobody ever has. But if people want to interfere in things that don't concern them, then they can easily come to a bad end.'

Without waiting any longer, Dibya strode forward quickly. In the darkness under the lychee tree, Shantilata stood for a while, shedding tears. She had never wept in front of other people. But in this dark solitude she was confronted with the reflections of her sorrows. Her whole sad life came and stood before her again. Darkness was the appropriate light for this vision. Her tears fell slowly on the dry leaves underfoot.

The sudden cry of a bat in the tree brought her back to earth. She wiped her eyes with her sari, and slowly returned home.

Once there, she took Arjun aside into a corner of the porch. She forced herself to smile and said, 'Arjun, do you remember talking about moving out of here? Why don't we do that? Let us give up our two rooms to these poor, displaced people. It might be of some help.'

Arjun smiled sadly at her.

'No, Mother,' he said. 'That won't solve any problems. If five families have to crowd into these two rooms, then they'll be at each other's throats in no time at all.'

'That's for them to worry about. Let's just get out of here. Who knows how long this chaos will go on? You can never bring yourself to ask any of these people to leave. And yet, how can you work on your thesis in the middle of all these people?'

'Yes, you are absolutely right there. I am tired of all this myself. Yes, perhaps we should go.'

'Right, go and arrange for a flat tomorrow.'

'Mother, you can't find a place in just one day I'll have to look around. Why are you suddenly so eager to go?'

'Never mind. You start looking from tomorrow. Oh, one other thing. So many of your friends have gone abroad for higher studies. Can't you do something like that?'

'Yes, I suppose I could, if I tried. But what will you do, if I go away?'

'Don't worry about me for a moment. I shall be all right. Maybe I'll get a job as a cook or something in some house. I'm sure I can manage quite well.'

A cheerless smile came to Arjun's face as he looked at his mother.

'You think you'll be able to live without me?' he asked. 'If I go abroad, it won't be a matter of a year or so. It will be for much longer. Can you stay alone for so long?'

'Yes, yes,' said Shantilata with desperate eagerness. 'I'm sure I can. To see you work well and make a name for yourself will be the greatest happiness of my life. Don't worry about me at all. I shall be fine.'

'I see. You are going to sweat out your days as a cook in some household, and I am to go off abroad to study! Do you think the goddess of learning is going to give me her blessings if she knows this? She's more likely to spit on me.'

'We can go into all that later, dear son. Right now, you must find a place to rent. I just don't want to stay here any longer than I have to. My son can easily earn a handsome salary if he tries. Why on earth should I have to suffer in my old age like this?'

'All right, I'll start looking tomorrow.'

*

Being homeless for the second time had not only made those affected dispirited—it had totally numbed them. There were no signs of sorrow in Haradhan's face. It was as if he had accepted this sort of thing as his fate. He had got hold of a bundle of *bidis* and kept on smoking them one after the other. That was his one consolation. Dhiren was mourning his son's condition. Prahlad had stretched himself out flat on the floor.

It was the children who kept on crying in a low, nagging monotone. Arjun could never stand the sound of children crying. He moved restlessly about from place to place. Seven or eight of the elder boys were sitting on the front steps. They were overcome with fury and resentment—but they could not think of a way out. Haran kept coming up to Arjun and making one impractical proposition after another. There was a Muslim cemetery a short way off from the colony. Haran felt it would be a good idea to occupy that place by force. The land in a graveyard could never be anyone's private property. So there should be no trouble about taking possession. Arjun just could not sit still in one place for long. Everything seemed unbearable. He kept feeling the unfortunate people were reproaching him with silent glances. As if they had come to this pass only because of his advice.

Haran came to sit by Arjun again, and whispered in his ear.

'What shall we do now? How long can we carry on like this?'

Arjun did not answer.

Haran tried again.

'You've done a lot. You went to the police station, to the lawyer—but nothing was of any use. How much more can you do? You have your own research work to do. Just give me a suggestion as to how to deal with these people.'

Arjun answered with some irritation.

'I don't know. In a few days mother and I will vacate our rooms. We'll go away somewhere. That's all I can do.'

'Yes, I suppose that's best for you. But even so, it will be such a crowd in this tiny place. Looks like it would have been a better idea to have settled with Kewal Singh. At least they could have got some money out of that bastard. Do you think we can go to him now and explain things to him, somehow?'

Kartik, Haradhan's son, had been together with Arjun

189

almost all day. He had hoped that somehow or the other, Arjun would find a way out of the impasse. Suddenly he could contain himself no longer, but burst out at the top of his voice, 'I'll set fire to that factory one day. By God, I'll do it. Let them send me to prison or hang me for it, if they want.'

Arjun stared at Kartik for some time. A tumult raged in his breast. Then came the explosion. Arjun stood up and said, 'Come!'

'Where to?'

'Come with me, all of you.'

*

Yes, look, just take a look at this young man now. His name is Arjun. Arjun has now grown taller than his body. He is bigger than his own breadth. His life now has overstepped the bounds of his own existence.

Arjun's eyes are flaming with resolve, his jaw hard, every muscle in his fine body come to life and waiting. He has made the decision.

Arjun picked up the crowbar lying next to the door and said in a hard voice. 'Kartik, Dinu, Gora—all of you who wish to come, come with me. Try and take a stick or a pole each and come along.'

'Arjun,' cried Haradhan in an agony of apprehension, 'what are you trying to do? Where are you rushing off to like this?'

'You can come with us too, Uncle, if you want to. All of you are welcome to join us. We shall go immediately and break that wall down. This very night we shall plant stakes into the earth there and build our houses again. Words are worse than useless, and we've spent enough of those. No one will come forward to help us. So we must repossess the land tonight—and from then on, we shall stand guard every night. We'll see what they can do.'

A tremendous uproar started. The boys started running around in search of weapons. Haran asked, 'But Arjun, do you think they'll let go very easily? They will definitely fight it out with you.'

'It's much too late to think of such things Haranda.

Why don't you come along with us also?'

'But what if there is a criminal case?'

'Very well then, we don't need you. You can stay back.'

Shantilata came running up to Arjun and took him by the hand.

'What madness has come over you Arjun!' she exclaimed. 'You can't go, you must not go.'

'Mother,' said Arjun quietly, 'please don't be afraid. I shall definitely come back to you.'

'Arjun, I shall die. I'll die tonight. Don't leave me tonight. Stay here, please...'

'Don't be afraid, Mother. I shall come back.'

Arjun turned to his companions.

'We are not going there to have a fight,' he told them. 'Do not lose your cool. Remember, we are only going to pull down that wall and re-build our houses. We shall not let anyone stop us. Understand? Come on then.'

They rushed down the front steps of the porch and advanced towards the pond. Grandfather Nishi was telling Naru a story before the child went to sleep. The noise of their passage brought Naru straight out of bed and near the window in one leap. The old man started groping in the darkness.

'Naru', he cried, 'where are you? What's all that noise?'

'Some people are going towards the factory.'

'Who?'

'There, there they are. Arjunda, Kartikda, Uncle Gora and all the rest. There is definitely going to be a big fight tonight.'

'Take me there, please take me there.'

'What do you want to go there for? You just stay here, I'll run along and take a look. Then I can come back and tell you all about it.'

'Dear God, Oh merciful God! Who else is there with them?'

*

The dog was running at Arjun's heels. Arjun tried to send him home once.

'Go back Becharam, go on back to Mother.'

But the dog would not leave. Then, suddenly, Arjun saw Labonya. She was running towards them, gasping for breath, a chopping knife in her hands. Her whole face looked abnormal. Arjun extended an arm to stop her.

'Where are you trying to go, Labi?'

Labonya cast him a fiery look and said, 'This is the end. I'll destroy everything today,'

Arjun still tried to stop her.

'No, Labi. Stop this madness. Go home.'

But Labonya raised her knife, turned to him with a threatening gesture and said, 'Don't you dare. Not another word out of you. I am going to put an end to it all today.'

'Why are you making trouble for us? You don't need to go at all.'

'I do need to.'

And Labonya started running forward, ahead of the rest. Arjun and his group started running too. Arjun carried the same crowbar which his unknown assailant had left behind after injuring him.

A row of faces confronted them from the other side of the wall. Arjun stopped short for a few minutes with his companions. He tried to get used to the darkness and make out the faces. Then he shouted, 'Move aside, Dibya, we have come to break down the wall.'

Dibya answered, ominously, 'I cannot allow anyone to damage the property of the factory.'

'You know quite well, this is not the property of the factory.'

'I am not prepared to take it from you.'

Labonya was struggling to move forward, but Arjun held her back. Kartik spoke out this time.

'If you try to stop us too hard, we'll set fire to your precious factory.'

'Go on, you fool, do your best.'

Inside his house, Grandfather Nishi kept asking questions. 'What's happening now, Naru? How many of them are there? Who are they? Naru, tell me...'

'I can't tell you. I can't see them any longer.'

'Then take me there.'

'What do you want to go into the middle of a fight for?

Listen, I can hear Dibya*da*'s voice.'

'Oh God!'

Arjun took one more step forward and saw, next to Dibya, Ratan, Shambhu, Nitai and two or three strangers. A little way off, stood Kewal Singh himself. All of them were armed with sticks. A conflict was inevitable. On his side, Kartik, Gora, Dinu and the other boys were getting restive, they were definitely spoiling for a fight.

Arjun tried again.

'Dibya, how can you go along with this attempt to make so many of your own people homeless? All this, just for a job? Why don't step aside—and we can come to terms with the factory owner.'

'Stop being pious. Go home and hide behind your mother.'

'Dibya, I beg of you. At least let these five families have one small piece of land each.'

'Shut up, you bastard. Who asked you to interfere?'

'Dibya, just because they have given you a little job—does that mean you have to take the part of those greedy people? And abandon your own kind? Please stand aside. Let us settle the matter.'

'I told you, if anybody dares to touch this wall, I shall break his arm.'

Labonya was shouting again.

'I'll put a stop to everything today, really end everything.'

'Come Arjun,' said Kartik, 'what's the use of talking to them any more? Let's move forward.'

But suddenly, Arjun was overcome by sorrow.

'No, let it be. Let it be for today. Let's just go back.'

'Go back? What are you saying? Have you gone mad?'

'What then? Shall we fight our own people?'

Arjun threw the crowbar down and covered his face with his hands. A terrible, helpless anguish tore at him. Just a few steps forward would plunge them into actual, physical conflict. Who knows how many would die, how many be injured? Arjun felt such a surge of power in his body that he knew he could easily tear apart the whole world now. But who were the people he was going to use his power on? Dibya, Ratan, Shambhu, Nitai—the same people with whom he had played in the colony as children. There had been so many occasions when he had gone home with them and eaten meals cooked by their mothers. Dibya's mother had been seriously ill for a long time before she had died. At that time, Shantilata had brought Dibya over to stay with her. That was a time when Arjun and Dibya had slept side by side on the same bed!

These were the people he had looked on as his friends and kin--was he to engage in battle with them today? Even Kewal Singh, he too was a fellow countryman. Was the price of land greater than the value of a human life? Wasn't it better to beg for alms for the rest of your life, than to kill your own people? Doubt paralysed Arjun with a trembling helplessness. What was he to do? What should he do now? There was nobody around who could advise him on the better choice. Different people just confused him by saying different things, but no one could show him the way out.

'What's the matter, Arjun? Have you lost your nerve?'

Even then, Arjun would not take his hands from his face. His companions were almost unable to restrain themselves any longer. Labonya was screaming something over and over again. And Arjun was still unable to decide what he should do. Agitation held him, trembling all over. An intense sadness flooded his being. All these friends and kin—to engage in bloodshed with them! What good was land at that cost? It was better to turn back.

A sudden, bestial howl shook him out of his trance. Kartik had answered his opponents' abuse with a really filthy expletive. In return, they had hurled a brick. The brick had been aimed at Arjun, but it had missed him and hit Becharam on the head. The dog lay on the ground, writhing in agony, his blood flowing in a copious stream.

A totally different kind of trance possessed Arjun at the sight of blood. A second brick came hurtling forward to hit Dinu on the shoulder. Kartik ducked as he said, 'Careful now, they may even have bombs. Arjun, Arjun...'

Arjun picked up his crowbar again. Now he was more

terrible than the most terrible of sounds. His whipcord-like body was taut as poised arrow.

'What is there to be careful about?' he roared, 'Come on, friends, break it down. Smash that wall, raze it to the ground.'

And whirling the crowbar over his head, Arjun leaped over the wall, crying, 'Come on, just try to stop me, you cowards. Come on, if you dare. I shall destroy everything today.'

XII

Who am I? Ahhh, I hurt all over. Have they tied my arms to the bed? No, my arms are free all right. But I can only lift my right arm, the left feels so heavy. My head—no there's no bandage there. They couldn't hit me on the head this time, then. My head's all right. I can remember everything.

My name is Arjun Raychoudhury. My father, my brother—yes, I remember their names too. Jute fields on one side, rice fields on the other, the raised path between them, the cremation ground beside the banyan tree, we burnt my father's corpse there, that whole rural image is not in the least bit blurred, it is luminous in my memory. I remember it all. Brother, I promise you, some day I'll go back there. And I shall say to them, we don't want a war, we don't want the five *bighas* of land we owned. Just give us a twentieth portion of that land and our tiny, ramshackle cottage—my mother suffers so, she can only find peace there. When the evening comes, my mother will go and light a lamp under the *tulsi* plant and blow on her conch shell. Brother, I give you my word, I shall go back one day. But I won't be able to take your dog with me. You told me never to chase him away. But those people have killed your Becharam...

Yet another injection! Nurse, nurse, there is pain all over my body, don't hurt me any more. Which hospital is this? I am so thirsty, can I have some water? Nurse, you have such a beautiful face, just like my mother's. But don't you be as sad as my mother. Keep your hand on my forehead a little longer—ah, how cool it is, how beautifully cool.

But I have bandages all over my chest and my back. They must have knifed me in my ribs. And I too... Have I killed a man? I lost all control over myself, I just wasn't thinking any more. I whirled the crowbar round and round over my head, and whoever came in front of me was... I felt a demonic strength in my limbs then. There was a face, a face with a close, thick, black beard... Did I hit him on the head? But, then, why did Kewal Singh raise his knife against me first? No, I promise I shall never set hands on a weapon again, ever. Yes, but to whom do I make the promise? To you, Mother. I promised you I would come back, haven't I kept my word?..

Who is it? Oh, it's Uncle Biswanath. Of course, I can recognize you. I haven't been hurt too badly. How is Labonya? Has she recovered? Ah, I do so hope she recovers soon. The poor girl has suffered so much. She felt she could not better her lot in life. But tell her to try again. Tell her, one should never give up, all through life. What? Did Labonya really plunge the knife into Dibya's arm? Did I hurt Dibya too? Oh yes, in his thigh once, with my crowbar... No, I have no anger against Dibya. If only he had not stood on the other side of the wall. Had he been on the same side as we were, then there would have been no fighting... I ask for forgiveness. Dibya, Kewal Singh—I ask all of you to forgive me. I do not want to hurt human beings. But what should I have done then? Nobody would tell me. Oh, I feel terrible, this pain, this pain in my chest, and this pain in my heart too.

Will Kartik be all right? And Gora? Uncle Biswanath, do stay a little longer. Don't leave me just now. Please look after my mother. Oh yes, I know you will, in any case. But I just felt like saying it. If we don't step forward to help each other in times of trouble... Just see to it that somebody forces my mother to eat. Tell my mother, I am being fed very well in hospital. They give me so many injections of glucose, that my stomach always feels full.

'Do you know something, Arjun? The government has finally taken up our case.'

'But how did they know about us? Who informed them?

Normally, it takes them ages to move.'

'The papers splashed it across in a big way. That professor of yours—he came with the reporters. Your picture was in the papers too.'

'I can't believe it.'

'And, listen, the government is going to give every one of us registered deeds of ownership to the land within the month. Which includes that disputed piece of land too!'

'I knew it, I knew it. Didn't I tell you all, you can get nothing unless you stand up and protest? Rights have to be taken. If we had let Kewal Singh have his way with that land, then soon all the members too...'

'Yes, the other members would have been evicted too.'

'Uncle Biswanath, you must tell Labonya to try again. Labonya wanted to rise above her surroundings. The pain of her failure... Why is there such a crowd around my bed? Nurse, do tell them, I can't stand crowds. I feel suffocated. Such a lot of noise, it is deafening. They don't seem to know that at least in a hospital they should speak softly. What, these people are the police! So, they want to put me in prison, do they? Let them. But now, I just want them to leave. Let them observe the rules of the hospital. What are you saying, nurse? No crowds? No noise? Then what is it? Am I going crazy? Very well, try holding up your fingers in front of me. How many? Three. There now, wasn't I right? How many this time? One. You see, my brains work all right. Why do you wear this coral ring, nurse? Do you have stomach problems? Oh I see, you are a Christian, and this is your wedding ring. But whoever heard of a coral wedding ring. Oh God, don't make me laugh. My stomach hurts abominably if I laugh... I think I'll sleep a little.

'Is that you, Abanishda? Do please sit down. I am much better now. I had a nap, and my head feels quite clear now. Did you say you'd come before? When? Yesterday? How many days have I been here, what is the date today? Oh no, I really have wasted a lot of time then. As soon as I get back home, I shall complete the thesis.'

'The way you are going, Arjun, I doubt if you will ever get to finishing that thesis. Who knows how long it will take you to get well!'

'Oh no, don't worry about that. I shall be fine. They wanted to kill me. But they'll never succeed. I'll live.'

'That's all you can say. In the space of two months you have got into two situations like this. Why do you have to get involved in this sort of thing? You should keep yourself busy with your research.'

'What's the use? All my life I have just kept myself chained to books and academic work. What good was that to me? What good is that to anybody?'

'Not to everybody, perhaps, but to some. If you had not studied chemistry, would you have known so much about the world of matter? With some people it is impossible to convey these truths, in spite of tremendous efforts. But since you can grasp them so easily...'

'Yes, but how can I bury myself in my books and ignore what is going on in the real world around me?'

'I am not saying you have to do that. But each person should do that which is best suited to his abilities. This country of ours needs all kinds of talents. It is just as relevant to learn medicine or chemistry as it is to eradicate poverty through organized efforts. There are some people who can break their heads against a wall, and still not be able to get a first class degree in chemistry. Let them do something else. But for you, it is different.'

'Yes, but when an external problem becomes very immediate, it is difficult to think like that.'

'All right, no use arguing about it now. Get well soon.'

'Oh, yes, that I shall. You'll see, in two or three days I'll...'

'There's no need to brag about your strength. Arjun, if I have to lose a boy like you, I shall be more sorry than I can say.'

'No, Abanishda, I shan't disappoint you.'

'Very well. Stop talking now, and go to sleep. I'll come and see you again tomorrow. Maya says she'll come with me then.'

*

199

I seem to be sleeping all the time. If I have a visitor, I can at least talk a little. Otherwise, if I just lie here alone, I seem to fall into a trance. If they have knifed me in the ribs, why does my head throb so? Maybe I should've studied medicine instead of chemistry; the mysteries of the human body seem more fascinating than the mysteries of the world of matter. But it costs a fortune to study medicine—besides, I wonder if I could have come out at the top in medicine, just through hard work. It is easy to do well in chemistry, that's why I chose it. But most people don't know that. Thank God, they could not hit me on the left side instead of the right. That would have been the end of me. But no, it's not so easy to kill me. Who else was supposed to come visit me? No, no one is supposed to. But it would be nice to get visitors—I do so feel like talking.

'Hello, Akhtar, do come in. Oh yes, I am fine. I almost feel like sitting up. Perhaps I'll be able to, tomorrow or the day after. Hasn't Shukla come with you? What? Oh, she is busy with her friend's wedding. Which friend? Nandita? I see. If I had been well, no doubt I would have been invited too. But, of course, Shukla always has something or other to keep her busy...

'You are leaving for Germany in four days time? I'm sure that will make Shukla very unhappy. If I'd not been laid up, I would have come to the airport to see you off. We could have made a real do of it. How long will you stay out? Three years! No, I won't go to Germany, I won't go anywhere. At the moment, I can only think of staying at the colony in Dum Dum. Yes, you are quite right, this is a bit of a pose I have, almost a gimmick—a slum boy with a first class Master's degree—how wonderful! Otherwise, there are thousands of boys like me. Every year, in all the subjects, there are first class degree holders...

'But what a pity you are going away. I won't be able to go to your house and eat *kebabs* any more. Your mother once made those mutton *kebabs*—ummm, wonderful. I can still taste them. I do sound repulsively greedy, don't I? To talk about food like this. This is what hospitals do to me—it seems like I haven't had a decent meal in ages.

Just glucose and glucose and glucose!

'Yes, I shall go to your house, even if you are not there. I'll ask your mother to feed me. Okay Akhtar, I'll see you when you return home. Bon voyage! Au revoir!'

*

Ahhh, God, how it hurts! I cannot turn on my side, I can't lift my head, everything is going dark. Nurse, have you forgotten me? What if everybody in this hospital just forgets all about me? What if I die without making a sound? Oh God, this pain is killing me. How can anyone bear such pain? But I must bear, I must live—there is still so much to do. I wonder why Uncle Biswanath looked so grave. Have the doctors told him I am to die? No, no, no, that can't be...

'Haranda, how did you break your arm? You have it all wrapped up in a sling. You weren't with us in the fight. Oh, I see, you had an accident in your taxi. I hope it is nothing serious. You see, Haranda, you went and broke your arm in a car accident. Yet, if you had come with us instead, a broken arm would not have made you feel sorry for yourself. You'd have been jubilant. Do you think I regret what I have done? Never. If I am in the same situation ever again, I shall do exactly the same.

'Haranda, why are you leaving so soon? What—a lady has come to see me? What lady?

'I knew it Shukla, I knew you'd come. However busy you may be, you'd still come.'

'How could you have known that?'

'Oh, I knew all right. Akhtar was here this morning. He said you were very busy with Nandita's wedding. When is she getting married?'

'She got married day before yesterday to Akhtar.'

'What? To Akhtar? And that wretched boy never said a word. So Nandita must be going with him to Germany?'

'Yes.'

'And I, like an idiot, said to him that you would be quite miserable because he was going away. He just sat there grinning. Well tell me the truth, aren't you a bit sad?'

'Of course I am. Stop talking such nonsense. Just lie

201

back and be quiet.'

'What is this? Are you going to tell me off, even in the hospital? Is it fair to scold a sick man? What will people say if they hear you?'

'Stop making fun of me. You really enjoy driving me up the wall don't you?'

'Come now, when have I ever done that? I haven't even seen you for the last ten days or so.'

'You just go around making trouble, and you expect others to remain untouched?,

'But I haven't made trouble. You say these things without knowing all about it...'

'Don't you try to fool me. I know all there is to know. Why couldn't you have talked to my brother or my father before you got involved in a brawl? You could have found out whether my father could do something or not.'

'Why on earth should I talk to your father? Do I have to tell him all about my domestic problems?'

'No, of course not! It is much better to get beaten up and...'

'Please, don't scold me any more. You shouldn't be so hard on a sick man. I could die of heart failure, you know. Haven't you got any perfume on today? Why don't I smell it?'

'Just listen to him! He's going to spend ten days out of the month in hospital with a broken head, and I'll have to come to him all dolled up with perfume on me, just so he can smell it!'

'No, of course you don't have to. It is much better instead to yell at me. And you certainly do that very well. Tell me, Shukla, have you cried, even once, in the last two or three years? I've always seen you happy, and having a good time. Though, you do become a bit aggressive whenever I am around. But I have never seen you cry. I would like to see what you look like when you cry.'

'You haven't seen it, because you don't have the eyes to see. Not every person sheds tears in the same way.'

Why, what has happened to me? I don't seem to be able to reply to Shukla at all! And why did she have to say this so suddenly? Her voice sounds unfamiliar too. I've never heard Shukla speak in such a soft voice.

'Shukla, what is the matter with you? Please tell me, do.'

'Nothing's the matter. And, anyway, you will never understand.'

'Have I offended you in any way, unknowingly? You are so angry with me today. But you know, I never wanted to bother you in any way. I am so far removed from your world—that is why I've tried not to encroach on you. You have such a beautiful life—I know I can have no place there.'

'Yes, and knowing that, you have to go and do these stupid things—break your head, or get stabbed in the ribs, and lie here in a hospital! You don't have the capacity to understand what torture I suffer at such times. I don't seem to be able to enjoy anything, I don't feel like going anywhere or seeing anybody; at night I can't even have the pleasure of sleep.'

'Why do you think you feel this way?'

'I don't know.'

'I know what it is. Basically, you are a soft-hearted person. You can never rest easy when you hear of the sufferings of others. I am really sorry to have upset you in this way.'

'Enough of that. Just remember one thing. I do not wish to remain indebted to anyone.'

'What do you mean?'

'Just what I said.'

'Please, dear Shukla, don't be so hard on me. I am in terrible pain all over. My head is not clear today. I can't quite make sense of everything. Please explain what you meant by being indebted.'

'I was about to drown, and you saved my life. Now do you think you can die just like that, and leave me indebted forever? I tell you, I won't have it.'

'Don't say such things. That was nothing. If I hadn't been around, someone else would have rescued you. How can there be any question of indebtedness? Give a paisa to any beggar in the street, that will absolve you of all obligations.'

'All right, you don't have to carry on babbling any

longer, you idiot.'

'You know, Shukla, that dog of mine, Becharam—he's dead.'

'Arjun! You are crying. Crying just for a dog!'

'My brother loved him very much. My brother...'

'Try not to think of such things now. Sleep a little. I'll go now.'

'No, wait. Listen, last time I reproached you for not coming to visit me in hospital more than once. It's true, I do feel a bit greedy—for I never get to see you all by myself at other times. Only when something has happened to me, do I—But anyway, you really don't have to come and visit me again. Don't come.'

'Why not?'

'Why should you waste your time like this, for no good reason? Besides, you must be so busy now. Akhtar and Nandita are going away, and they are such good friends of yours.'

'I came to see you yesterday and the day before. You had not recovered your senses then. I'll come again tomorrow, morning and evening, day after tomorrow, morning and evening, and the day after and the day after—'

'Why?'

'Just because I want to. Just because I feel like it.'

Ah, how good it is to be alive. What joy! Why do men court death then, why do they want to kill their fellow men? Nurse, please help me sit up a little. There is no pain in my chest any more, my head feels clear—I'll live all right, I shall live. I love being alive. They wanted to kill me, but I won't die.

From childhood onwards, death has come to me many times. When we left our country, I could have died so many times on that hazardous journey. In Khulna, when those two men tried to grab my mother, or at Sealdah station where so many boys died of cholera like flies. Even after coming to live in the colony...

These last two times, they wanted to kill me. But they'll never succeed. Never ever. I will survive. Yes, certainly I shall.

Glossary

apni	— Respectful term of address-You
arati	— Worship of idol by moving a lamp around it
babu	— As suffixed to name-Mr
bidi	— Cheap cigarette of rolled leaf
bigha	— Measure of land area—about ¼ hectare
Boudi	— Elder brother's wife
da	— As suffixed to name-elder brother
dhobi	— Washerman
dhoti	— Loose garment worn, wound around the lower part of the body, by men.
di	— As suffixed to name-elder sister
hilsa	— Savoury sea-fish also found in larger rivers
Holi	— Hindu spring festival
jamdani	— A typical Bangladeshi sari
Jethima	— Father's elder brother's wife
Kakima	— Father's younger brother's wife
Kabab	— Ball of roasted minced meat
Khurima	— Father's younger brother's wife
kohl	— Black powder used to darken eyelids
kotki	— A typical Oriya sari
natchgar	— Dance hall
neem	— Margosa tree
paan	— Betel leaf
Pishima	— Father's sister
pucca sahib	— Real gentleman, used sarcastically
puranbari	— Old house
Rangapishima	— Aunt
sadhus	— Holy men
shalik	— A species of mynah
shankhachur	— King cobra
tulsi	— Basil
tumi	— Informal term of address-you
zamindar	— Landlord

Glossary

appa — Respectful term of address–You

avval — Worship of idol by moving a lamp around it

aaya — An unfixed to name–Ma

Bidi — Cheap cigarette of rolled leaf

bigha — Measure of land area–about a hectare

Bhai — Elder brother, s wife

da — As suffix to name elder brother

dhobi — Washerman

dhoti — Loose garment worn wound around the lower part of the body by men

di — As suffix to name elder sister

hilsa — Savoury sea-dish also found in saltwater rivers

Holi — Hindu spring festival

jamun — A typical Bengali dessert sweet

jethima — Father's elder brother's wife

kakima — Father's younger brother's wife

kabab — Ball of roasted minced meat

khurima — Father's younger brother's wife

kohl — Black powder used to darken eyelids

Kurta — A type of loose shirt

kartagan — Dinner guest

neem — Marubá tree

paan — Betel leaf

Pishima — Father's sister

chupa o sobn — Keral term for sari, specifically

Pregnant — Childless

Panaspirunam — Aunt

Sadhu — Holy men

sunka — A species of snyati

Rani-capital — Gha, Pista

uka — Bird

tuma — Informal term of address–you

samjhate — Landlord